ELUSIVE LEGACY

In the early years of the nineteenth century, England and France were at peace, but the coming of a Frenchman to the Devonshire village of Challiscombe was to have a far-reaching effect on several people's lives. With the stranger's arrival came intrigue, death and a swift change of circumstance for Louise Vaughan, causing her to become aware of dark violence hidden in the past. Setting her future happiness at risk, Louise made a desperate bid to seek out the truth.

Books by Kathleen A. Shoesmith
in the Linford Romance Library:

BRACKENTHORPE

KATHLEEN A. SHOESMITH

ELUSIVE LEGACY

Complete and Unabridged

LINFORD
Leicester

First published in Great Britain in 1976 by
Robert Hale & Company
London

First Linford Edition
published 1997
by arrangement with
Robert Hale Limited
London

British Library CIP Data

Shoesmith, Kathleen A. (Kathleen Anne), *1938*–
Elusive legacy.—Large print ed.—
Linford romance library
1. Love stories
2. Large type books
I. Title
823.9′14 [F]

ISBN 0–7089–5188–0

Published by
F. A. Thorpe (Publishing) Ltd.
Anstey, Leicestershire

Set by Words & Graphics Ltd.
Anstey, Leicestershire
Printed and bound in Great Britain by
T. J. International Ltd., Padstow, Cornwall

This book is printed on acid-free paper

1

THE sea was calm, a shimmering expanse of pewter-grey, in imitation of the early morning sky above. Until a pinkish glow, heralding sunrise, rippled across both sea and sky, all was still, the silence absolute. Yet, even as a first glimpse of fiery orange showed above the headland of the bay, the air was rent by the outraged shriek of gulls. The seabirds rose, it seemed, from nowhere and soared aloft. Eventually some of their number descended to the water and bobbed there with watchful dignity. Others wheeled downwards, intent on discovering the despoiler of the morning peace.

Up on the cliff top, half-hidden by prickly gorse and sparse, tough clumps of grass, was a boy. He was lying on his stomach, chin resting pensively in his cupped hands, eyes fixed hopefully in the direction of the headland. Slowly the greyness was replaced by a gentle blue of sea and sky and across the rippling water slanted orange rays of sunrise. The boy waited until the bright orb of the sun was suspended in its entirety in the cool blue of the sky. Then, with a sigh, his purpose accomplished, he began to move away from his vantage point. Suddenly he was still, his eyes sun-dazzled. Someone was down there on the beach. It was the familiar stooped figure of eccentric old Caleb Vaughan. On the point of calling to attract the old man's attention, the boy paused. Vaughan had waded up to his waist in the sea and was dragging something from the spiteful clutch of the chain of rocks. These rocks formed a rough causeway which partially divided the bay.

With a grimace of distaste, the boy watched Caleb Vaughan move shorewards, hauling behind him a small battered boat. His stomach lurched as

Vaughan pulled what could only be a dead body from the craft. The old man deposited his limp, unresisting burden on the beach, then began to search it for booty. His hands stilled at a faint cry and he turned as a smaller figure emerged and stumbled out of the beached boat.

The boy rose to his feet and watched in fascination as old Caleb Vaughan hesitated, then scooped up the small form in his arms and made his way across the wet sand to his cottage on the cliff side. Sitting down again thoughtfully, the boy stared for a long moment at the still, dark shape on the beach beside the ramshackle boat. Then he turned his head to look at the footprints which made a deeply indented track towards old Vaughan's cottage. He waited, torn by indecision, but the old man did not reappear.

"What do you mean by this, young sir?" came the sudden demand of an ill-tempered voice.

The boy rose with a start, to face his

irate tutor. The hour was far advanced and he must be late for morning studies. Explaining that he had left the house to watch the sunrise, would bring sarcastic comment, but it seemed imperative that he should speak and divert his tutor's attention from the beach. If the unmoving object down there were truly a corpse, then old Vaughan would report its presence at his leisure. The boy did not relish the prospect of being dragged down to investigate the nauseous sight personally. He stepped hastily away from the cliff edge and, with a show of reluctance, admitted to the unmanly sport of sunrise-gazing. As he had anticipated, his tutor greeted this admission with disgust and lectured him all the way home on the unwisdom of peculiar pursuits.

"Emulate your brother, young sir!" he was advised. "You may be sickly and prevented from joining him at school, but this does not mean you should indulge in moonstruck fancy!"

The boy was relieved to be safely away from that tell-tale scene on the beach and he refrained from defending his morning's excursion. Ill-health had consigned him into home-education and his tutor's oft-repeated aim was 'to make a man of him'.

Yet, sickly or not, the boy contrived to climb from his bedroom window that night, in order to walk through the darkness towards Caleb Vaughan's cliffside residence. The morning's events had intrigued him. It had not been moonstruck fancy that had witnessed the old man on the beach! It was to be hoped that Vaughan had removed the corpse from the tides' clutches, mused the boy, but his interest was not in the dead man.

A sloping pathway led down from the cliff top to the cottage, which perched on an outcrop of rock. The pale light of a solitary candle flickered at a partly-curtained window, enabling the boy to look into the cottage's one room. The interior was familiar, for he had known old Vaughan from childhood days. It was sparsely furnished and left much to be desired in its state of cleanliness.

The old man was seated in a chair, one horny hand clutching an empty pipe, the other resting upon the shoulder of a small girl who was sitting at his feet. In the uncertain light, it appeared that she was perhaps eight years old and that she possessed an abundance of curling dark hair. Yet, however poor the visibility, there was no mistaking the absolute trust in the wide childish eyes directed up at Caleb Vaughan. The boy gazed in for a long moment, his thoughts racing and then turned quietly away, pondering on what he had seen. He left the cottage and went up the sloping cliff path.

It was a dark, moonless night in late spring of the year 1793 and when an unseen nocturnal animal startled him, the boy became tardily aware of possible danger. His country had been at war with France since January and only a stretch of water separated him from those barbarous enemies, who had executed their own king. The truant scholar had a more retentive memory than his tutor supposed and he began to shiver as he recalled lurid details heard of France's Revolution. Greedy *Madame Guillotine* was the chosen method of execution and she was continually avid for fresh victims. Firmly the boy told himself that it was extremely unlikely that a desperate fugitive from the Terror would be abroad in the surrounding darkness of the Devonshire countryside. Nevertheless, he hastened his steps, breaking into a headlong run when heavy drops of thundery rain began to fall. He ran until he was breathless and was soaked to the skin by the time he reached the sheltering porch of his home.

Too wet and filled with sudden, nameless dread, to effect a secret entry, he pounded for admittance at the heavy oaken door, until his father's dogs roused the entire household by howling above the noise of the rumbling thunder.

After being confined to his bed for a week with a feverish chill, the boy escaped his tutor's vigilance once more. As before, his aim was Caleb Vaughan's cottage. He found the old man painstakingly spreading a small black gown upon his gorse-bush drying ground. The boy watched silently for a moment, then called out:

"Caleb! Hello!"

Old Vaughan turned, his wrinkled, sea-tanned face wary. He seemed to relax when he saw only the boy.

"Good day to you, young sir, m'dear," he mumbled. "You'm found me at my wash-day, see."

The boy nodded, as if unsurprised by this singular event. He indicated the wet garment on the bush.

"I saw you on the beach last week," he said hopefully, "with a little girl."

Caleb Vaughan cast an uneasy look behind him as the cottage door opened and a child appeared. She was wearing only a tattered shirt of Caleb's and her

8

dark curls were tousled. She looked at the boy curiously, then gave an urchin grin. Her eyes were of a very deep blue and were thickly fringed with long black lashes. She opened her mouth to speak but remained silent when Caleb spoke hastily.

"Get you inside, m'dear" he cautioned. "You'm catching your death not proper-dressed, an' that!" He straightened stooped shoulders and scowled at the boy.

"You saw me on the beach, young sir? Doubtless you'm wondering 'bout that dead 'un I found? Don't you fret! Vicar's promised to give 'n a Christian burial. Now, go your way, young sir. I'm busy an' we've work to do, me an' Lou."

"Lou?" persevered the boy. "Is that the child's name, Caleb? Who is she?"

Old Vaughan lifted his chin with proud defiance.

"She be my li'l maid," he said firmly. "Her folks are dead an' I'm her Granfer. She's come to live wi' me, has my li'l Lou."

The boy accepted the information gravely, but he was plainly dissatisfied. About to question further, he was interrupted by an irate shout from the cliff top.

"So you are here, sir ! I have scoured the countryside to find what keeps you from your studies. I did not expect to see you conversing with peasants!" The tutor drew in his breath with an angry snort and added sarcastically, "Perhaps you will introduce me to your friend?"

Impulsively the truant scholar turned to give old Vaughan a broad wink.

"I apologise for causing concern," he said to his tutor. "I was obliged to visit my old friend, Mr. Vaughan."

"Obliged? *Obliged*?" demanded the incensed tutor. "What is amiss with the fellow that you should absent yourself from the schoolroom without permission?"

The boy looked from his teacher to old Vaughan.

"Why, nothing is amiss," he declared innocently. "I came to pay a social-call on my friend Caleb and his — his grandchild."

Still grumbling, the tutor led him away. Caleb Vaughan put an arm about the small girl's shoulders and stared up the path at the boy's retreating back. The relief and gratitude in the old man's faded eyes were not unmixed with apprehension. He hugged the child to him.

"You'm hungry, Lou," he said. "Granfer'll get you a bite to eat."

They entered the cottage together and the door closed behind them.

2

IN the adventurous days of the 1580's, a certain seacaptain named Reginald Challis was, by reason of his outstanding valour, dubbed knight by his gracious monarch, Queen Elizabeth. "We bid you rise, Sir Reginald" was still ringing loud in his ears, as he rode off to his home county of Devon. It was said later that his horse had been startled in some way for he allowed himself to be unseated and broke the bones in both of his legs. The injuries healed in time, but the new Sir Reginald was forced to admit that his sea-going days were over. Accepting his fate stoically, he proceeded to order the building of a home worthy of his improved status. He chose to have a manor-house, built in the new, unfortified style close to the southern coast of his native Devonshire. Much pleased with the finished result, the injured hero married a child of half his age, who was sole heiress to her father's wealth. Three short years after the gaining of his knighthood, Sir Reginald was in possession of a gracious family home, a wife of leisured means and ample riches of support — his wife's father having considerately died — and two small sons to perpetuate the name of Challis.

A nearby coastal hamlet, as yet unnamed, grew to accommodate the family dependants of servants at the Hall and so Challiscombe village came into being.

It became custom that the heirs to Challis Hall should wed young gentle-women of wealth, thus providing additions to the splendour of their family home. Elegant furnishings, elaborate tapestries and fine porcelain, made the manor-house a dwelling of note and distinction.

Yet, in the year 1776, the present elder son, Reginald, attempted to go against tradition by unwisely declaring undying love for a young female of gentle birth but less than moderate means. To the relieved satisfaction of young Reginald's parents, the young lady of his affections proved unworthy. Without explanation, she eloped with a French nobleman — France and England were then briefly at peace — and failed to return the items of family jewellery rashly bestowed upon her by the besotted youth at their secret betrothal.

Feeling the end of his world had come, the Challis heir was persuaded without difficulty into marriage with a young lady of his parents' choice. She was endowed with sufficient wealth to suit custom.

A year went by and the old father was obliged to die without the pleasure of a grandson at his knee. When the embittered Sir Reginald finally accepted that the love of his life had gone forever, he grudgingly paid a little attention to his neglected young wife, only to discover her amiability and timid desire to please him. Deciding to make do with second-best, he gradually came to look upon poor Cecilia with affection and was dismayed when she died after giving him twin heirs.

More affected than he cared to admit by the death of the woman to whom he had given so little, he defied tradition once more, by refusing to name the first-born twin, Reginald. The babes were christened Gerard and Piers and they thrived amazingly, although the younger displayed a sad sickliness throughout childhood.

The proud father lavished his unstinting love upon his heirs, belatedly filled with guilt at his neglect of their dead mother. Twenty-one years went by and the Challis twins grew to manhood. Plans for a celebration for the double coming-of-age were made, months before the anniversary in August. No expense was spared and the Long Gallery, beloved of the Elizabethans and now condemned as draughty and difficult to heat, was transformed into a ballroom.

Despite the fact that this important occasion fell in summertime, fires were lit in the gallery's two hearths from the beginning of July and the decorative plaster ceiling was carefully cleaned so that woodsmoke could not deposit itself on existing grime.

It was decided that the many small-paned windows along the length of one side of the gallery should remain uncurtained. The window-seats and the straight-backed chairs, purchased in 1730 by the present owner's father had been re-upholstered in dark red velvet. The effect of an expanse of polished wood floor, warm-coloured velvet, light ceiling and sparkling window-panes was very pleasing to the eye and the whole staff of servants basked in the pleasure of their master's satisfaction. The gallery was to be illuminated at great expense by hundreds of wax candles, in wall-brackets and chandeliers above the window recesses and between the portraits on the opposite length of the gallery.

★　★　★

"No one'd think 'twas war-time wi' all *this* lot!" protested a village man who had been brought in as extra help at this busy time. "So this is how rich folks live! You'd think young masters'd be wantin' to fight for their country an' beat ole Boney at his game, 'stead o' havin' fancy parties!"

"Rear-admiral Nelson don't need no mere boys to do his work!" scoffed the head stableman, who had spent his life in service of the Challis family. "Got ole Bonaparte on the run, has Nelson! Destroyed the Frenchie's fleet last year, didn't he? What more d'you want? My guess is as ole Boney's hiding still in 'gyptian parts."

"Shame pressing seems to have stopped," went on the village man, nursing his grievance against the rich.

" 'Twould have done your young sirs

17

a power 'o good if press-gang'd carried 'em off for a spell o' naval service!"

"You'm crazed!" uttered the stable-man in disgust. "There be no finer shot nor swordsman in all Devon than our two young masters here! Get out o' my sight, numskull! Go see if there's a chance o' a sup and a bite from the kitchen. Fair parched my throat it has, listening to your ravin'. You'm here to help me while young Jim's busy moving chairs and such about inside the Hall. Go on! Earn your wage and wangle a drink and some food from Cook!"

The villager, a tall thin fellow with a lame leg, left the tables and limped to the kitchen door, wiping dirty hands on the seat of his leathern breeches. He was met at the door by a young servant-girl, clad in an enveloping white apron. Dark hair was pushed severely beneath a starched cap, but a curl had escaped on to her smooth brow. Lively enquiry in her dark blue eyes, suggested that she might be more approachable than the unbending Cook.

"Er — um, excuse me, missy," he began. "Mr. Trant has sent me from the stables. He'd like some ale an' a bite to eat, if you'm not too busy."

The girl gave a soft laugh and nodded her head down at the laden tray held before her.

"Sam Trant'll think the pixies told me!" she said, her speech clear yet holding the familiar Devon burr. "See, it's here already! There's ale and bread and cheese and — oh, yes, an apple for my own good friend. Come I'll let you carry the tray! Mind now," she cautioned gaily, "for 'tis heavy. Old Sam do like his bread and cheese cut generous!"

The bemused man limped in the girl's wake, the tray held carefully in his large hands and he marvelled to find himself obeying this pert slip of a maid. He had lived in Challiscombe for but six weeks and would forget his intention to move on, if all the lassies here were like this one.

"Not so fast, young missy," he

muttered, hoping she would fall into conversation with him. "See — I've a lame leg, an' that."

Blue eyes surveyed him across an aproned shoulder and the girl gave a shrug.

"Seems to me you'll find your way back to the stables without my help!" she observed briskly, as if to set him in his place. "Now, take the tray to old Sam, do, for I have an appointment with milord Jasper and Cook will be vexed if I'm not back in the kitchen soon."

Intrigued by her manner and aggrieved by what he termed her 'fine lady airs', the man, Frederic Smith by name, thrust the tray at the waiting stableman and limped off to discover the identity of 'milord Jasper'.

Thinking herself unobserved, the girl had pushed back her cap to reveal dark, curling hair. Smith watched her offer the apple on her small flat palm to a wicked-looking black horse. A bad-tempered brute, that was, considered the villager from unpleasant knowledge of the creature. Belonged to one of Sir Reggie's twin heirs, it did. Never reckoned to see it so docile-like, pondered Smith as, apple eaten, the black horse suffered the girl to rest her cheek against its smooth neck. She started and adjusted her cap quickly when Smith lounged round the stable doorway and stared at her from watery, pale-blue eyes.

"What be your name, my pretty one?" queried the man, as he contrived to block the doorway with his bony frame. "I be Fred, see, an' I know that brute's temper. You'd do well to leave off stroking it an' gi' *me* a kiss instead!"

He took a halting step towards her and grinned unpleasantly when the girl stiffened and thrust a disdainful chin in the air. Liked 'em with spirit, he told himself.

"Well, I should be back in the kitchen, not talking here with you, Mr. — Mr. Fred," she said primly, wondering if she might dive to safety under his arm.

Frederic Smith came nearer, a hopeful grin on his hollow-cheeked face.

"Just one li'l kiss an' I'll let you pass, m'dear!" he promised, scowling when the girl gave him a look of undisguised distaste. "You'm too good for the likes o' me? Is that it, my grand miss kitchen-maid?" he demanded, lunging out with one large hand to grab at her shoulder.

With a lithe twist of her slim body, the girl ducked beneath his hold and made for the doorway. Smith, never steady on his lame leg, faltered then stumbled against the questing nose of the great black horse. Then, with a gasp of pure terror, the man fled, pushing past the girl, his amorous intent forgotten.

"Oh, Sam! I'm glad to see the back of *that* one!" said the girl with relief, when she heard footsteps coming in from the stableyard. "I'll not visit milord Jasper again, till *he's* left the Hall and that's a fact! I think — oh, you're not Sam!" She gasped and fell silent before the level regard of an amused pair of grey eyes. "You'm Mr. Challis?" she asked, after a long moment, then added foolishly: "Well, *one* of 'em, I reckon?"

She had been employed in the kitchen of Challis Hall for almost three years but had never, until now, been face-to-face with either of Sir Reginald's twin heirs. Until recently, the two young men had been absent from home, completing their education. There had been much speculation in the servants' hall about the looks and nature of the young masters. Remembering this now, the girl flushed and dropped her eyes. However, her loss of composure did not prevent a quick assessment of this young man's undoubted handsome appearance. Then, with a hasty, embarrassed movement, she straightened her cap until it hid her dark hair.

The gentleman (Mr. Gerard or Mr. Piers?) was frowning thoughtfully and she fidgeted uneasily beneath his scrutiny, knowing she should go but prolonging this, her first meeting with one of the young masters. She wished suddenly that she had been clad in something more becoming than her kitchen uniform, then suppressed this thought as foolishly unsuitable. Why, she did not even live in the same world as this finely-dressed gentleman!

Even as she stood before him, poised for flight, he held out his hand and offered her a devastatingly attractive smile.

"Yes, I am one of the Challis twins," he said lightly enough, but his regard was uncomfortably searching. "You are — ? You *must* be — ?"

"I — I work in the kitchen, Mr. Challis, sir," she whispered. "I must go, or Cook'll have my hide!"

She fled without a backward glance, only pausing in vexation to retrieve her cap which fell to the ground in her haste. Her embarrassed discomfort was out of proportion, mused young Challis, as he watched her slim figure disappear into the kitchen-quarters. He gave his horse, Jasper, an absent pat, then went with an air of purpose to seek out Sam Trant, the head stable-man. It seemly oddly important that his surmise should receive verification.

"Come you in, m'dear," said Cook, her sarcastic voice deceptively gentle, as she eyed the truant maid. "Took your time about it, didn't you? You're a lazy li'l slut, an' that's a fact."

No more was said, but somehow the girl's tasks that day seemed to have multiplied. She shrugged philosophi-cally. Extra work was a small payment indeed, for the morning's encounter! Fat old Cook would not sneer at me, if she knew I'd met one of the young masters, thought the girl, as she scrubbed the kitchen table with her customary vigour. There was no point in getting on Cook's wrong side though, she pondered. Her job in Challis Hall's kitchen was important, for there was not just herself to consider. With a sigh, she dried her reddened, work-worn hands and moved on to the next task.

★ ★ ★

The coming-of-age celebration party was proceeding as smoothly and successfully as could be wished. The gravelled drive, neatly raked in the early afternoon, was now churned up with wheel tracks and the stables were filled with carriage-horses belonging to invited guests. In his room above the stables, Sam Trant was entertaining rarely-seen cronies who were employed as coachmen to the visiting gentry. Down below, the lesser stablemen were sharing ale and cold pie, but Sam was tasting wine from his master's cellars tonight. Sir Reginald had been generous on this, the coming-of-age of his twin heirs.

Inside the manor-house, the long gallery was proving an ideal ballroom, with hired musicians at one end and favoured upper servants discreetly dispensing light refreshment from a room at the other end. Mr. Gerard, the elder twin, had assured his father that a formal supper would be desperately old-fashioned. Sir Reginald smiled to himself as he considered his son's protest. The master of Challis Hall was seated now with his younger brother, Thomas, who farmed a considerable estate in the wilds of far-off Yorkshire and had travelled the many miles with his daughters to attend the important family event.

"I told Gerard that this new-fangled continual buffet-arrangement wouldn't work, Thomas," remarked Sir Reginald in the satisfied tones of one proved correct in surmise. "See how everyone is holding back until supper is properly announced!"

Mr. Thomas Challis felt bound to agree and nodded gravely. He had seen only young Gerard and his friends taking any form of refreshment. Everyone else appeared to be awaiting permission to eat.

"I'd best have a word with the servants," said Sir Reginald, with a good-natured smile. "They were not exactly in accord with Gerard's idea and a change of plan will suit everyone."

Mr. Challis watched his brother, a fine figure of a man, if somewhat portly in his rich coat and the old-fashioned wig he always wore on dress occasions. Sir Reginald paused to exchange civilities with his guests and was then joined by the younger twin, Piers. Mr. Challis approved of what he knew of his nephew, Piers, although he was usually hard-put to tell the twins apart. When his young relatives were together, it was Gerard's gayer manners and careless ways which identified him to the puzzled onlooker. Yet they were so alike in their enviable youthful grace, those boys of Reginald's. Thomas was glad, he told himself, only half-convinced that *he* had no difficulty recognising his three dissimilar daughters apart. There was little point in sighing after the son he had never had, he told himself firmly, when he had three motherless girls to settle in this world. He rubbed his chin thoughtfully, as his eyes took in the pleasing sight of young Gerard persuading his girl-cousins to form a set for an Elizabethan country-dance.

For a moment, Mr. Challis lost his habitually mournful look and gave a half-smile. His nephews would come in for a sizeable inheritance one day and must already be considered well-worth the cultivation of local matchmaking matrons! Well — those boys could do worse than look within their own family for wives, nodded Mr. Challis sagely.

Piers Challis listened to his father's proposed alteration of supper arrangements and promised to deal with the important matter himself. There was no reason why Sir Reginald should miss even an instant of the festivities, he suggested.

"Indeed, sir, you had best rejoin Uncle Thomas," he said with a grin.

"The speculative look upon his face tells me he is watching my brother flirt with our cousins *and* is thinking that an early marriage would do Gerry no harm! I can read his expression from here!"

Piers smiled as Sir Reginald went back to Mr. Challis with more haste than dignity. The smile faded as the younger twin acknowledged the obvious sense of seeing Gerard's attentions fixed with Priscilla, Marianne or Sarah. Family rumour held the notion that the unsurpassed wealth of Uncle Thomas' dead wife had been kept more or less intact, for the sole purpose of providing enviable dowries for the cousins. Piers shrugged. Gerard was the elder twin! On *his* shoulders must rest the traditional task of marrying an heiress! It seemed there was, after all, some advantage in being the younger son, mused Piers gravely.

One quick word aside to the awe-inspiring Wentworth, whose word was law in the servants' hall was all that was required to change the refreshment arrangements and Piers watched for a moment as dishes and chairs were whisked into more appropriate positions and men servants lined up behind the main table to serve the guests. He suspected that the all-seeing Wentworth had been prepared, from the onset, for a formal supper!

Piers was about to return to the dancing in the gallery, when he became aware of the stillness of one of the lesser maidservants. Everyone but this girl seemed to be scurrying efficiently here and there beneath Wentworth's dignified direction. The fact that she alone was motionless, served to emphasise the way in which she was staring at Piers from wide blue eyes. She turned and fled from the room when he cast her an enquiring look. After a moment's consideration, he filled a plate with tempting morsels then casually left the supper-room with a nod of approval to Wentworth.

Instead of returning to the gallery,

Piers went through a series of rooms which led one from the other, until he reached the head of the stairs leading to the kitchen-quarters. He had moved quickly and his quarry was now in sight. Her white-aproned figure was ghostlike in the flickering light of a candle and she halted uncertainly, biting on her lip, when he bade her be still.

"You dropped your cap again, child," chided Piers with an encouraging smile as he held out a crumpled piece of starched linen, the laden plate threatening to spill its contents at any moment.

She murmured thanks and took the cap, frowning at the careless way in which he held the food. This was the same young man she had seen this morning, she thought suddenly. He was even more grand and unapproachable in his well-cut evening clothes and she marvelled that she should have met him twice in one day. *What* precisely did he propose to do with that mountain of food? She could hardly tear her fascinated gaze from the dainties he held.

"You are Caleb Vaughan's granddaughter, I believe?" he asked. "No — stay a moment, Louise! That *is* your name?" he added, when she clutched the wooden stairrail and descended two steps in her eagerness to leave him.

"Cook'll have missed me, sir," she said in an unsteady whisper. "An' you'm not to worry yourself about us. We do very well, Granfer and I."

Piers frowned at her flushed cheeks and unhappy blue eyes.

"You do not enjoy kitchen-work, Louise," he said quietly, "and why should it be expected of you? Yet where *do* you belong, child? What shall be done about you?"

Slowly she came back up the stairs.

"Sir — you'm fuddled with wine," she suggested, attempting a smile. "Where should a kitchen-maid belong, if not in the kitchen?"

"A kitchen-maid!" said Piers musingly. "It will not do! It will not do at all" With a sudden, brusque movement, he thrust the laden plate of food at her. "Oh — these are for you, child. You look half-starved! Don't let Cook take them from you, either."

He turned abruptly from her, his eyes angry in the candlelight.

"Well — thank you, Mr. Challis, sir," murmured Louise dazedly. "I'll save these good things as a treat for Granfer. He's been ill and I reckon he'll prefer these tasty things to his usual bread an' cheese! You'm very *kind* to us, sir," she added gratefully.

Piers Challis rejoined the party which was half in his honour, yet knew he had not been missed. To all intents and purposes, Gerard alone was their father's heir. *He* was but the younger son, for all that they were twins. Yet even younger sons possessed a certain influence, he decided, as he led Cousin Marianne into the supper-room. Courteously he dealt with his cousin's refreshment, but his thoughts were of the aproned ghostlike figure at the head of the kitchen stairs. Already he had found an answer to the easiest way of improving the situation, without causing undue comment.

"Cousin — do you expect me to *eat* all of this?" asked Miss Marianne Challis in mock-alarm. "I vow I thought you'd never stop! I trust you will carry it to our table? I am sure that I will disgrace myself by dropping it all over the carpet!"

Piers lowered his eyes in surprise at the enthusiastic amount of food with which he had just presented his smiling cousin and he had the grace to flush. A benign glance from the lordly Wentworth caused his colour to deepen further and he hoped the manservant had not remarked the empty-handed return which had followed his first onslaught upon the supper-table.

Thomas Challis gave a nod of satisfaction as he linked the sight of his daughter, Marianne with her hot-cheeked cousin. If the conclusion that good gentleman reached fell wide of the mark, at least he kept this fresh hopeful sign to himself. Piers would have been horrified to read his uncle's thoughts but, mercifully, had no inkling of them.

3

"I TRUST you expressed proper gratitude to Sir Reginald?" said Mr. Parswell, vicar of Challiscombe and surrounding hamlets. "This is indeed a change of circumstances for you — ah, hum — yes, Louise. Your master is all goodness. Few great men of his position would unbend to the extent of educating a — ah, a kitchen-maid." He glanced at the flushed cheeks of the soberly-dressed girl who was sitting in obvious discomfort on the extreme edge of a chair in the vicarage library. "Ah, but you no longer serve in quite so humble a capacity, I believe."

"N — no, sir," admitted the girl quietly. "I have been instructed to work at plain sewing with Mrs. Vernon, the housekeeper. I left the kitchens last week." She was evidently ill-at-ease and overawed by her good fortune and the vicar nodded in self-satisfaction when she added: "I just cannot *think* why Sir Reginald should ask you to teach me, sir. There's no reason for even a *sewing*-maid to be educated!"

Mr. Parswell beamed at her in a fatherly manner and Louise experienced further amazement at her change of circumstance. It now appeared that, in addition to her removal from the Challis kitchen, she was to spend two hours each morning receiving tuition from the vicar. Even more astounding was the fact that her considerably less arduous duties would mean the elevation of her wages by an extra three shillings a week. The full extent of her improved situation was beyond all expectation. True, she had always hoped to rise higher than the kitchen one day but, this — *this* held more promise of happiness than she had ever dared wish! Soberly she acknowledged now the vast relief she had felt on being removed from the power of the sadistically soft-tongued Cook.

"Yes, sir," she told the smiling vicar, her voice unsteady. "I am truly grateful to the master an' I hope I thanked him properly. You'm not to think I forgot to thank him!"

Mr. Parswell looked at the girl's cheeks, flushed now with an excess of amazed gratitude. The dazed expression in her dark blue eyes confirmed that his faith in Sir Reginald's good sense should not waver. It was not unnatural that the vicar should have produced many dubious mental reasons for his patron's singular kindness to a humble kitchen-maid and the girl's undoubted good looks had done little to dispel his doubts. But her humble gratitude and surprise were genuine enough, nodded Mr. Parswell in relief. For all his certainty that she was not romantically involved with his patron, he hoped she would not speak unwisely of the increase in her wages. Kitchen-maids' earnings might be meagre, yet to give the girl three *shillings* more each week must surely invite speculation! Sir

Reginald had explained his generosity by declaring bluffly that the child seemed to have no clothing other than her kitchen-uniform and that she had an aged relative to support. Mr. Parswell nodded sagely to himself. If his patron had erred by giving the girl too much, then he, as her teacher, must see that she learned the value of money. Like as not, the 'aged relative' — one Caleb Vaughan, of doubtful reputation — would spend the whole of it on drink, if matters went unchecked!

No — it was apparent that his unworthy guess had been completely wrong. This child had not found favour in her master's eyes! The vicar had been prepared to avert scandal, even to the extent of losing his living in Challiscombe — a disagreeable thought. His relief knew no bounds. Sir Reginald's name had never attracted a whisper of doubt in *that* direction, in all the twenty-one years since the death of his lady. It was plain that it would take more than an undernourished kitchen-maid to tempt that good gentleman from the narrow path of respectable conduct. No — this was merely a whim on Sir Reginald's part. No doubt the master had noticed the girl's intelligence, compared her age with that of the vicar's daughter, Millicent, and decided that two were as easily taught as one!

Mr. Parswell let out pent-up breath in a quivering sigh and Louise Vaughan looked at him curiously. She had no way of knowing that the vicar was stooping to the very worldly occupation of comparing the protegée's undoubted beauty with his own daughter's looks. At thirteen Miss Millicent, was a sweet, good girl, but only passably pretty.

Lessons at the vicarage opened the new pupil's eyes to a world far beyond all hopes and in less than one week, Mr. Parswell became aware of a desperate thirst for knowledge in his young student. He blessed his wife's sensible upbringing of their only daughter. Millicent had a gentle nature which precluded all jealousy of the newcomer's looks and superior intelligence. Indeed, the girls seemed on the way to becoming fast friends, although the sewing-maid never presumed upon her position and deferred to Milly's wishes without question. The vicar marvelled that Louise should prove so apt a scholar. She appeared to possess no living relative, save old Caleb Vaughan — a fellow reputed to have once belonged to an unsavory wrecker-gang in Challiscombe Bay. Investigation had revealed Vaughan to have left the village some thirty-five years ago, to return later, minus the wife he had wed in his absence. Yes, it was not only possible, but highly probable, that this child was his grand-daughter. Her intelligence must stem from her grandmother's side of the family, decided Mr. Parswell shrewdly.

It was clear that Millicent liked Louise and Mrs. Parswell, a semi-invalid for several years now, could speak nothing but praise of Sir Reginald's protegée. Louise worked diligently at her lessons and quickly became proficient in arithmetic, English grammar and — surprisingly — the French language. Already she had a more convincing French accent than little Milly, although this accomplishment would be useless to her in her role as sewingmaid. After much deliberation, Mr. Parswell suggested to his wife that Sir Reginald had noted the girl's undoubted intelligence and chosen to equip her with the qualifications necessary for a governess, or even, a teacher, for Challiscombe was without a village-school. Perhaps Sir Reginald intended to endow a charity-school one day in the future?

"It would be a pity if Louise never rose beyond servant-status," agreed Mrs. Parswell in her gentle, kindly manner. "She's a willing child and quite without conceit. She has even made progress away from her countrified manner of speech. I think she models herself on Milly, my dear. Have you noticed the way she watches her at table?"

"Ah, I have indeed!" beamed the vicar. "I feel that our little one is also learning from Louise. Already, Millicent is becoming more self-reliant and puts forward her own opinion when we hold schoolroom discussions. I am pleased that they have struck up a friendship."

The days went by without outward event, but to Louise Vaughan each day was touched by its own special magic. She was seeing life beyond the cramped conditions of mere employment and enjoying every moment of this new experience.

She rose early and attended to the needs of her old grandfather, smiling at his childlike pride in her scholastic ability. Never of a religious turn of mind, he had, none the less, produced an old Bible from amongst his possessions and delighted in having his 'clever li'l maid' read aloud to him.

Her lessons at the vicarage at ten o'clock in the morning, followed four hours work at Challis Hall, but she was too excited with the prospect of bettering her position to admit to tiredness. For the first three weeks of her new life, the girl hurried back to the Hall when lessons ended at midday, partook of a hasty luncheon, then sped to resume her duties in the housekeeper's room. On seeing Louise becoming gradually thinner and paler of cheek, Mrs. Parswell altered matters with a gentle word in the necessary quarter. From that time, it became practice for Louise to take luncheon at the vicarage, a simple yet well cooked-meal, which was eaten at midday. Although she was at first alarmed to realise her afternoon work had been reduced in this way by at least half an hour, the girl was reassured to find her superior, Mrs. Vernon, in complete accord with the new arrangement.

"No," she said graciously, in answer to Louise's stumbling query, "do not look so troubled, child. Sir Reginald takes an interest in your progress and most certainly will not deduct half an hour's work-time from your wages each day. You are a very fortunate girl," she concluded, with a heartening smile.

Comparing this lady's very different outlook with that of Cook's despotic rule of the kitchen, Louise showed her gratitude by persevering with her 'plain sewing' to such an extent that she was judged capable of the exacting task of repairing the young masters' fine linen shirts. Smoothing an invisibly mended collar with her thumb, she pondered occasionally on her two meetings with one of the young masters. She had not set eyes on either of the twin heirs since the coming-of-age party, but one morning in early October one of the young gentlemen deigned to pay a visit to the vicarage schoolroom.

Louise fell prey to furious conjecture. She had always been of the opinion that the improvement of her position stemmed from her meeting with one of Sir Reginald's twin sons on the night of the celebration-party. *He* had said she should not work in the kitchen and now she no longer did so! It had seemed more than likely that *he* — for some reason or other — had been instrumental in her receiving education. For this, she would stand in his debt for ever more, although her thanks must, of necessity, be given to his father.

When the handsome, self-assured young gentleman with the Challis looks, entered and gravely inspected the school books of Milly Parswell and herself, Louise wondered if here might be an opportunity of showing she was sensible of the honour she had received. When Millicent was sent to hasten the maid's preparation of refreshment for the guest and the vicar seemed immersed in the corrections he was inserting in Sunday's sermon, Louise grasped her failing courage, coloured becomingly and offered young Mr. Challis a shy smile.

"You seem to be an apt scholar," commented that gentlemen as he handed back her book. "I am sure you must be worthy of my father's interest!"

Louise cast Mr. Parswell a quick look. He was frowning over his sermon and she knew that Millicent would soon return with the maidservant and refreshment.

"I — I do my very best to justify his interest, sir," she whispered, then emboldened by his encouraging nod, rushed on: "I will be grateful to *you* for all of my life!"

At this point, the vicar rose to greet his daughter and the little maid, Agnes, who between them were carrying a tea-tray and plates of tiny cakes. Louise hurried to make herself useful and bent over the tray to hide her heightened colour.

"Ah, but there is wine, young sir, if that is more to your taste," beamed Mr. Parswell. "You are of age now, my boy, and I dare say tea is no more your beverage than mine, at this hour of the day!"

Gerard Challis gave his host an absent nod, but his attention was still upon Louise Vaughan and she would have been surprised, had she interpreted his grey-eyed look as one of speculative amusement. It sounded decidedly, thought Gerard gleefully, as if brother Piers had arranged the ascent of this pretty little thing from the kitchens! Now who would have thought *that* of his dull dog of a brother? The elder twin had not troubled himself with his father's odd whim of educating a kitchen-maid. He had merely assumed that the old man was in his dotage and his own inheritance was on the horizon. Only idle curiosity and time lying heavily on his hands, had led Gerard Challis to visit the vicarage today.

He had always considered his brother as a less lively shadow of himself, yet it seemed that his twin had a secret interest in this demure little beauty. Ah-ha, thought Gerard, an unholy gleam in his eyes. It was evident that the girl set the improvement of her position at Piers' door! It was also obvious, pondered Gerard, that she thought *he* was Piers! Sometimes it was a nuisance that they should appear so confoundedly alike, but today it might be turned to advantage. The young heir to Challis Hall was bored and this piquant situation promised a little entertainment!

Louise left the vicarage after luncheon and turned to wave her hand to Milly Parswell who was hovering at the door. The schoolroom hours and the honour of eating at the vicar's table were the highlights of her day and she never ceased to marvel at her good fortune. She skipped a few steps down the winding lane which led from the Parswell home to Challis Hall, a happy smile upon her face. Autumn sunshine gilded the turning leaves on the hedge-row and she paused to pick a late blackberry. This morning had offered an opportunity of thanking Sir Reginald's son for his kindness! She bit upon the berry, although she had just eaten, then made a wry face and tossed its sourness aside. She shivered and drew her shawl about her shoulders. The sunshine had deceived her into thinking it was still summer, but there was a nip of frost in the air. On the way to her cliffside home this evening, she would be wise to gather extra sticks for the fire. Granfer was still far from well and, at his age, he needed all possible warmth. It was a pity she had to leave him alone all day, she thought, but they could not exist without her wages.

She quickened her steps, then paused to nod in a friendly fashion, as a man came suddenly into her path round a bend in the lane. Halting with an exclamation of surprise, she recognised him.

"Oh — Mr. Challis!" she said with a small laugh. "You startled me, sir!"

"Learning to talk like a lady, are you not, little Miss Vaughan?" said Gerard Challis, who had discovered a little about her before leaving the vicarage that morning. "But for me you would still be slaving in the kitchen m'dear!"

She eyed him uncertainly.

"Y — yes! Oh, yes, indeed, sir!" she agreed, wondering if he had drunk too freely of Mr. Parswell's wine. He seemed about to mock her gratitude and a hurt frown drew her dark brows together. "I must hurry, sir," she said, attempting to pass him. She bit her lip in vexation when he sidestepped, a teasing grin on his handsome face. Pleadingly she added: "Sir — I am employed by your father. Do not make me late back. I cannot take advantage of his kindness!"

"*His* kindness?" he demanded. "I thought you wished to thank me for *mine*! Why else would I wait here for you? Oh — very well, go on your way."

Gerard Challis seemed about to let her pass, but moved when she moved and set a light kiss upon her lips. The girl stared up at him, all colour leaving her cheeks and for an instant she swayed upon her feet.

"Now, do not try to ape your betters by swooning at so mild a kiss as *that*!" scoffed Gerard. "Come, girl, you can thank me now for my kindness." When she still gazed at him in mute distress, he said impatiently: "Then get back to your work — it seems you are fit for nothing else! Don't stare as if you have never been kissed before!"

Louise stumbled on towards Challis Hall, her eyes bright with unshed tears, her fond illusions shattered. It did not occur to her to doubt that this unpleasant encounter had been yet another meeting with 'her' Mr. Challis. His seeming inconstancy made her unhappy for the rest of that week, as she tried to solve the puzzle of how he could be, at the same time, both cruel and kind.

★   ★   ★

Some days after the incident in the lane, Louise arrived at the half-open door of her cliffside home, to face the horrifying sight of her grandfather, Caleb Vaughan, lying full-length across the little cottage's one room.

"Granfer?" she stammered, fearing he had suffered a heart-seizure. She fell on her knees beside the still figure and lifted the old man's grizzled head on to her lap, to stare in disbelief at her stained hands. Caleb was bleeding sluggishly from a frighteningly large wound at the back of his head and his bearded face was ashen. She cast a terrified look about the room she always kept so neat and clean. Chaos met her unsteady eyes. Granfer's chair and her own small stool were upturned, the old man's bed was ripped apart and the curtain which closed off her sleeping alcove hung drunkenly from one ring.

It seemed incredible that a thief should deem it worth his while to search their humble dwelling. Caleb must have surprised the intruder. How *could* anyone attack a sick old man?

Catching sight of the treasured Bible, flung aside and stained with Caleb's blood, she shuddered violently and began to weep. The tears dried on her cheeks when, unbelievably, there was a slight movement and Granfer fluttered his eyelids weakly. He was not dead, after all. Joyfully, carefully, Louise put a pillow from the disordered bed beneath the old man's head, stared at him for a long hopeful moment, then ran headlong out of the cottage and up the sloping path, shouting aloud for aid, before it was too late.

It seemed both strange yet natural that her plea should be answered swiftly and by one of the Challis twins. Neither knowing nor caring whether the gentleman was Mr. Gerard or Mr. Piers, Louise grasped his hand as he dismounted and in quivering, incoherent tones begged him enter her home.

Caleb Vaughan was conscious now and seemed to be making a vain attempt to raise his head from the pillow, his lips silently framing a desperate query. The girl bit back a sob and fell on her knees at his side once more, taking one hand of her sole frail relative in hers and chafing it gently, as if her action might bestow some of her youthful strength upon the injured man.

"Granfer!" she choked. "I am here. Do not try to talk. Just be still and we will get Mr. Beckwith from the inn. Good as any doctor, they call him."

The old man moved his head in slow negation and Louise lifted incredulous blue eyes to meet the pitying grey ones of young Mr. Challis. Surely Granfer was not already past help? She tried to rise to her feet to demand that Beckwith be brought from the inn, but Caleb's hand gripped hers with a vigour that stayed her action.

"Nay, 'tis too late for any doctor, Lou-love," he whispered. "I know I'm done for. I've seen death on others well enough to know it's come a-claiming me now. You'm my pretty li'l maid — my li'l gift from the sea — don't leave me now — " He coughed and she wiped a smear of blood from his trembling lips, forcing herself to recognise that his end was indeed at hand. Caleb was talking again and she made herself listen, as the dying man's urgency filled her also. "He asked me 'bout *you*, Lou, but I told him nothing — *nothing* 'bout my own pretty li'l maid. But his face — his face was — "

Mr. Challis bent over the old man, one well-cared-for hand resting lightly on the girl's shaking shoulders.

"You saw the face of the man who did this to you, Caleb?" he asked quietly. "You'll be avenged of this, never fear, my old friend. Tell me who he was and what he wanted to hear about your grandchild. I promise you he will not go unpunished for this deed."

"I remembered his face — " murmured Caleb Vaughan indistinctly. "'Twas like that in Lou's — in Lou's — "

"In my *what*, Granfer?" asked Louise

57

gently. "But, no — it cannot be important. I beg you, sir, let him rest! Do not worry him with questions."

The old man's eyes flickered open again and he gave a travesty of his usual grin.

"*Rest,* is it then, my li'l maid? I've not led as good a life as I might've done — not till the sea gave you to me — but I reckon my Maker'll not deny me *rest* enough, when I've done wi' all o' this! Hold your tongue, my li'l love — time's gettin' short — " There was silence and Louise held her breath so that she might hear if her grandfather still breathed. "Ah, yes," went on Caleb Vaughan, "I remember now. He was like the man in your li'l picture, my Lou."

Mr. Challis lifted an enquiring brow at Louise, but she shook her head wearily.

"I've no picture, Granfer," she said. "I'm sure this is not good for you. Now, heed me, I beg of you! Rest a little and then," she gulped back a tear.

The old man was very weak by now and his faded eyes were closed, but he made the effort to open them once more and lifted one quivering hand to point vaguely up at the smoke-grimed ceiling.

"Up there," he whispered urgently. "Up there wi' Lou's box. Never told you 'bout that day the sea gave me you — changed my life, did my li'l love — my li'l maid — "

Caleb Vaughan had spoken his final words and his head dropped sideways on the pillow, only seconds after his pointing hand had fallen limply to the floor. Louise gave a dry sob and turned her eyes in entreaty to Mr. Challis.

"He's gone, hasn't he, sir?" she said dully, almost composedly. "His last words were ones of love to me, b-but I did so little for him, when I planned to d-do so much. I thought that when my education was over, I would get a better position and improve our h-home and b-buy rugs and perhaps even a new roof s-so that the rain wouldn't get in over the window and — what are you *doing*, sir?"

The young man turned to give her a reassuring look. He was standing on the solitary chair and one outstretched hand was probing into a small aperture where the roof met the uneven stone of the cottage wall. With a soft exclamation of satisfaction, he withdrew a cloth-wrapped bundle, then shook his dark head as a cloud of plaster and dust descended on him.

"Caleb wanted you to have this, child," he said quietly. He climbed down from the chair, wiping dirty hands on his coat, which was stained with the old man's blood, and went on: "He pointed up here, did he not? Well, here in this bundle, is something belonging to you — unless I mistook his meaning."

The young man deposited his find on the floor beside the girl, ran a hand through his dishevelled hair and smiled encouragingly. Louise stared at him in fascination. At her grandfather's command, this finely dressed gentleman had made himself positively dirty — so dirty that her first instinct was to ignore everything save the importance of fetching him water and a clean cloth. Slowly she rose to her feet, not even looking down at the still figure of the old man, so ominously limp upon the cottage floor.

"Sir — I'll get you — " she began unsteadily.

"You will open this bundle and fulfil Caleb Vaughan's last wish," said Mr. Challis firmly. "Then I will go to tell my father what has happened. Come, Louise, open the bundle and stop fussing about a little dust. This is not the first time in my life that I have been dirty, child!"

She still stared at him, motionless now with the shock of her relative's death. Then with a moan, she fell on her knees and cradled the beloved, lifeless form of the old man against her breast.

"Granfer, oh, *Granfer*!" she whispered brokenly. "You were attacked because of *me*!"

Mr. Challis sighed and shook his head, then bent over and pulled the cloth of soiled, faded velvet from the bundle. Revealed now upon the cottage floor, lay a heavy metal-cornered box and a smaller object which rolled a short distance and came to rest against the chair. Had old Vaughan died to protect these two hidden items from prying eyes? Could it be mere coincidence that this bundle had been concealed up there? The dying man's pointing finger had *seemed* to indicate that place where roof met wall. The girl, it was evident, was suffering from reaction at the old man's cruel fate. She was totally indifferent to the discovery of the bundle's contents, yet they might serve to distract her from the full realisation of her loss. The poor child, thought the young man compassionately, was now completely alone in the world.

"Look, Louise," he said persuasively. "Look, it seems to be a locket." He rubbed the small object on his ruined coat, then dangled it by its chain. "Gold — if I am not mistaken," he nodded. With relief, he saw the stunned expression replaced by a frown on the girl's smooth brow and she relinquished her hold on her grand-father's body.

"Come and see it, child," he said firmly.

Louise sat back on her heels and colour came into her ashen cheeks.

"You think Granfer was shielding the hiding-place of his — his treasures, sir?" she asked quietly. "If that locket is really gold, then it cannot be mine — or his, for we are but poor folk, as well you know."

The locket did not respond to the young man's attempt to pry it open, although it seemed likely that the trinket contained 'a li'l picture' of a man whose looks had been shared by Vaughan's attacker. The box, too, was either locked or sealed with the grime of age. With an exclamation of self-condemnation, Mr. Challis set down the finds and propelled Louise's resisting figure from the cottage and out on to the cliff-path. Despite her protests, he lifted her up in front of him on his black horse and took her, at a smart trot, to the village inn. Without wasting unnecessary words of explanation, he put her into the care of sensible Annis Beckwith, the innkeeper's wife, then proceeded to take full charge of the situation. The puzzle of the box and locket were not important in comparison with the urgency of communicating the fact and manner of Caleb Vaughan's death to Sir Reginald Challis. The master of Challis Hall was a Justice of the Peace. The task of discovering the identity of the old man's killer was his alone, but the younger Challis took it upon himself to arrange with the vicar for the burial of the luckless victim of attack. It would be a long time, mused Mr. Challis with anger, before the stunned expression in Louise Vaughan's blue eyes ceased to haunt him. He had been an unfeeling fool in prolonging her ordeal, by speaking of the box and locket across her relative's corpse, yet those items seemed strangely important, for all she repudiated all knowledge of them. Unless the approach of death had dulled old Vaughan's awareness past reason, then that concealed bundle held some clue to Louise's former existence. Despite the gravity of the situation, young Mr. Challis owned to an overpowering interest in the stubbornly closed locket and box.

It did not seem necessary to mention these discoveries to Sir Reginald and that gentleman, with much shaking of his head, decided that the attack on old Vaughan had been an act of panic by a would-be thief surprised by the frail owner of the cottage. Doubtless the killer was now many miles from Challiscombe. There seemed little chance that he would be apprehended

and brought to justice and no likelihood of a satisfactory explanation of
what had taken place that evening in
the cliffside dwelling.

Annis Beckwith cared for the bereft
Louise until the day of her grandfather's funeral, when a more permanent
arrangement was resolved. As the girl
stood, stony-faced, beside the open
grave, a sympathetic hand gripped hers.
A half-uncaring glance proved her
companion to be Millicent Parswell
and when the vicar had concluded his
intonation of the traditional words, the
younger girl whispered:

"Of course you will live with us now,
Louise! Mama approves of the plan and
agrees that I am in need of a
companion. We are capital friends
already, are we not?"

Milly's firm decision and reassuring
manner reached through the icy chill
around Louise's heart and she found
that, after all, she could try to smile her
gratitude. Granfer would have been the
very last person to nurse a desire for

revenge, realised Louise unwillingly. He was dead, but life — for her — must go on.

So Caleb Vaughan's grandchild took up permanent residence in the vicarage and the circumstances of her relative's death robbed even the more callous of her acquaintances of the opportunity of envying her good fortune. Indeed, Challiscombe in general, heaved a sigh of relief to have the problem of the girl's future taken from the shoulders of the village. She was a fine good girl was old Caleb's Lou. Vicar had shown sense in giving her a home. It was something he would not regret.

The cliffside cottage and its contents, together with the sealed locket and metal-cornered box were now, indisputably, Louise Vaughan's possessions, but the only legacy she wished from her grandfather was the memory of the undoubted love he had held for her. Time would blunt the keenness of her grief and the horror of her discovery of that day in October. She locked up the cottage which was her only remembered home, recalled young Mr. Challis's interest in the locket and box and went indoors again to collect them, although they meant nothing to her. She knew now that the twin who had shown good sense and kindness in her time of need, had been Mr. Piers. That *he* should be the owner of her favourite horse 'milord Jasper' was a slender enough reason for deciding that he was 'her' Mr. Challis, but she was convinced that the gentleman she had met in the stables and on the night of the coming-of-age party was Piers and to be trusted. *He* had never bestowed that scornful kiss upon her, nor mocked her pretensions to ladylike behaviour. Mr. Gerard was the culprit there and must be avoided at all costs! Yet, pondered the girl with unwonted sadness, it was scarcely likely that avoidance would be necessary. In her humble capacity as dependent of Mr. Parswell's generosity, her path might never again be crossed by either of Sir Reginald Challis's heirs.

4

IN March of the year 1802, Mrs. Parswell ceased her earthly suffering and was laid to rest in Challiscombe churchyard. It was noted by the village people that the vicar had taken the death of his wife 'mortal bad'. It was not to be expected that little Miss Millicent, at fifteen years old, should take on the role of housekeeper to her widowed father. Milly Parswell was well-liked in the village, but not even her closest acquaintance judged her capable of running a household. Took after her poor dear mother, for uncertain health, it was said.

It seemed not only natural, but obvious, that sensible Louise Vaughan should manage affairs and direct the two housemaids about their duties. Opinions on Miss Vaughan varied. Some people thought she had accepted the vicar's charity for quite long enough and that, at almost eighteen years of age, she should be thinking of taking up paid employment outside of the vicarage. Why should *she* live like a lady with Miss Millicent, when her old granfer had been nothing but a wrecker and a smuggler in his youth?

Yet Louise had many friends in Challiscombe and she never grew too grand for *them*, they declared stoutly. Never mind *whose* grandchild she was, she had the manners of a lady now and spoke clearly and elegantly like quality-born. Indeed, Annis Beckwith, the innkeeper's wife, had even begun to wonder if her friend might one day become Miss Milly's step-mama — although it was too soon to put *that* hopeful thought into words. She was a good lass, was young Lou, nodded kindly Annis. The girl had helped with the running of the vicarage as Mrs. Parswell grew steadily weaker. Of course, she must play housekeeper at least until the vicar's natural grief had abated. Still, there was no harm in mental matchmaking, thought Annis sagely. Vicar was still on the right side of fifty and little Lou could do worse than wait and let things run their course!

Louise Vaughan was completely oblivious of Mrs. Beckwith's hopes for her future. Housekeeping came easily to her and she seemed to have an instinct for dealing with the maid-servants in a manner both firm yet friendly. They showed no resentment and both Mr. Parswell and Millicent seemed to take for granted her position in the household.

Three years had gone by since the death of Caleb Vaughan and, true to her supposition, Louise had had little contact with her benefactors, the Challis gentlemen. The old man's death had left a gap in her life, but she had successfully filled this with putting her energy into the task of making the vicarage a happy home for all of its inhabitants. She had not enquired after Caleb's death, of any financial arrangement between the vicar and Sir Reginald and had, at first, continued to work for Mrs. Vernon, the Challis housekeeper. Now that her duties were confined solely to the vicarage, she still received a monthly sum of money, but was able to set much of this aside, as her needs beneath the vicarage roof were considerably less. From time to time she wondered if she should question the source of her wages, but always decided that the time to do this was now past. If the money came from Sir Reginald, then it was up to *him* to cease payment. If it was paid from the vicar's own pocket, then she could only hope that her work gave satisfaction. At least now she was officially the vicarage housekeeper, she could attempt to repay her true debt to Mr. Parswell and Milly — the debt of kindness she had owed them both since her time of need: a kindness which could hold no monetary measure.

It was now late March and the spring sunshine, after winter's gloom, was almost as welcome as the news that the protracted war with France was over at last. It seemed that everyone, except the former Prime Minister, William Pitt, was heartily tired of war and its restrictive grip on foreign trade. Certain necessary household goods had become steadily less available and if Mr. Pitt's resignation last year meant an end to this war and the opening-up of fresh avenues of trade, then house-keeper Louise Vaughan was in full accord with that gentleman's decision! Politics were only rarely discussed in the vicarage. Mr. Parswell's interest was in past history, rather than present strife and his sermons seldom concerned themselves with the worldly difficulties of wartime and household management in this trying time. To his young housekeeper, as to the women of Challiscombe, the word peace was synonymous with the lowering of the price of wheat from its ridiculous elevation of sixteen pounds the quarter. Bread could now begin to take its natural place in the daily menu once more!

"But do not think we must be extravagant and waste good food, Carrie," scolded Louise gently, as the younger maid hastily scooped up a dropped loaf, hot from the oven, and prepared to discard it as unfit for consumption. "Cut off the top crust, by all means, but do not throw out the whole of it for the birds! I vow we have the fattest sparrows in all Challis-combe!"

"Yes'm — I mean, Miss Louise," stammered the girl guiltily.

How prim and housewifely I am becoming, thought Louise ruefully, as she went up to her own bedroom. Carrie is scarcely younger than I am, yet here I am — scolding away like a cross old woman! If the fattest sparrows are found in the vicarage garden and their plumpness comes from thrown-out crusts, then *I* am probably more at fault than anyone! There was something so pathetic and waif-like about sparrows that served to emphasise one's own good fortune, mused Louise profoundly.

She stood for a moment, looking with pleasure round the room which had been hers since she came to live beneath the vicar's roof. She loved this small apartment, which was upon the same floor as Millicent's and its equal in old-fashioned comfort. Grief-stricken by the death of old Caleb, she had found sanctuary in this warm and friendly room, with its heavy polished furniture and its intricately worked patchwork quilt. It was her own private domain and no one entered without first knocking at the door for admittance — except Carrie or Agnes in the course of their daily cleaning tasks. This small haven had done as much as dear Milly or Mr. Parswell to deaden the pain of the manner of her relative's death.

Louise knew that she performed her

housekeeping duties well and was happy enough, but sometimes felt obliged to rein in an unworthy desire for something from life, other than her present lot. When this momentary yearning would not be denied, she always comforted herself with the thought that soon Milly must learn how to run the household. The vicar's daughter was by no means the frail child she appeared!

"I am happy here," whispered Louise in the stillness of her room, "and yet — When the time comes for Milly to take charge of affairs here, I might discover more to life than is now apparent. Somehow I cannot see myself staying just *so* for ever! I will *not* become old and grey before I have *lived*!"

She clapped a hand to her mouth to stem the ungrateful admission, but the words had been said aloud for the first time and she gave a shrug and refused to wish them unsaid. Not for the whole world would she give pain to her benefactors, but instead of praying forgiveness for her temporary ingratitude, she went to stand before her mirror and appraised her looks carefully. Her own familiar reflection stared gravely back at her and she acknowledged without conceit that she had been blessed with looks a little out of the common. Her eyes were of a wide, clear blue and they tilted at the corners, mocking at her elderly occupation of housekeeper. They were fringed thickly with long black lashes and she accepted that they were probably her best — if not her only good — feature. Her nose turned up slightly at the end and her jawline was too firm to be really feminine. Yet her mouth often gave the impression that a smile lurked there beneath the outward severity.

"And my teeth are whole and even!" she retorted, surprised to be making so lengthy an assessment of her personal attributes. "I have work to do and yet I'm standing here and noting my best points like a horse going to market!" With a sudden urchin grin, she looked again into the mirror. "Why should I not be frivolous — at least for an instant longer? It is quite an entertaining pastime!"

Then, as she exchanged glances with her reflection, her smile faded and her hands crept up to grip her upper arms as she was seized by a sudden, inexplicable chill. The image in the mirror seemed to alter before her staring eyes. It blurred as if wet with rain — or tears — and she swayed upon her feet, caught up in an emotion she could not understand. When the reflection steadied and sharpened into focus, she saw that in some frightening way she had become older. The woman — herself — looked sadly at her from eyes of paler blue; her cheeks took on a lined careworn pallor. Her hair was dark, yet somehow unkempt and different in style.

Louise gripped the edge of the dressing-chest until her knuckles showed white, as her mirrored self took on an even stranger cast of feature. For perhaps a second — a fleeting instant of time — she saw a handsome man of middle age. His eyes matched hers for depth and brilliance of blue and his brows and lashes were black as her own. His hair, in contrast, was so devoid of colour that it seemed he must be wearing a wig.

With a moan of painful protest, the girl rubbed fiercely at her eyes to dispel mounting terror and, when she dared to look again into the mirror, saw her own ashen-cheeked image. Far from reassured, she sank limply on to a chair, weak with emotion and half-swooning.

"This is — is ridiculous!" she whispered eventually. "I am quite alone in the room, but those people were here and not entirely in my imagination! Somehow they were not strangers either. Each, in their way, was familiar to me and yet — Who are they that they should share my looks and my mirror? Who can they be, if not a part of my own shadowed past, come to haunt me now?"

She had no clear memory of her early childhood and Caleb Vaughan had always explained this odd gap of recollection, by referring to the dreadful illness she had had before he brought her to live in Challiscombe. Granfer had told her never to strain to remember the past, for it held nothing but unhappiness. Her poor parents had died of the same disease which had afflicted her.

Louise paced her bedroom, hands tight-clenched, yet shivering no longer. There had to be a rational explanation for the images seen in her mirror! Perhaps those two people had once been known to her, yet why should they show themselves to her now and in this unsettling manner? She gave herself a mental shake and vowed not to speak of what she had just seen. If she should reveal that she was seeing *visions*, the superstitious village people would shy away, muttering darkly of witchcraft!

I must be overtired, she thought,

seizing gratefully on this sensible explanation. Yet, tired or no, why should those strange reflections hint at a violence similar to that of Caleb Vaughan's untimely end?

The odd experience troubled the girl deeply. During the afternoon of that same day, she suddenly remembered the box and locket she had brought from her grandfather's cottage and the old man's dying murmurings of a face like the one in the 'little picture'. The locket had cleaned up beautifully and had proved to be of delicately chased gold. She wore it as her sole ornament, but had never attempted to force it open to discover if it did indeed contain a picture of any kind. Rough treatment would render the trinket useless and, until now, she had never really believed that the locket was originally hers. She thought of it as a gift from her kindly old grandfather and wore it for his sake alone.

The small leathern box with its metal corners had seemed of little value and had opened beneath the pressure of a kitchen knife, a month after Caleb Vaughan's death. Eagerly she had looked inside, to find its interior disappointingly empty. It held no clue to the forgotten past. In all likelihood, Granfer's pointing finger had meant nothing and Mr. Challis' finding of these two items had been sheer coincidence.

That night, Louise had a dream which was disturbingly real in its intensity. She was standing alone and helpless in a room filled with noise, movement and colour. Faceless men appeared from nowhere to swoop with cries of fiendish glee, snatching up and bearing off the richly attired ladies and gentlemen who fled from their path. The cackles of inhuman laughter were still ringing in her ears, when she woke with a start and found herself safe in the vicarage. She was bathed with perspiration and gentle Millicent Parswell was hovering anxiously at her bedside, a candle in her hand.

"D-did I waken you, Milly?" stammered Louise breathlessly. "I am sorry! I must have had a — a nightmare."

"This is unlike you, Louise, dear," said Milly in a troubled voice. "Come, tell me what you dreamed. Share it with me and perhaps then you might sleep more peacefully! Your face is white as a ghost and your eyes the size of dinner-platters!"

Louise was obliged to laugh at the younger girl's choice of words and she said lightly that she must have eaten something which had disagreed with her.

"Do not look so concerned, Milly," she begged. "I assure you, I am quite well. Let us go down to the kitchen and I will make us each a hot drink. My dream is forgotten, but my heedless panic in the dark has set *you* in a tremble! It was unkind of me to frighten you so."

Quickly she got up from her bed, donned a wrap and took the candle from her friend's unsteady hand.

"We are so close, you and I," said Millicent shyly. "I was fearful that you would be ill!"

"I am quite well, love!" repeated Louise stoutly. "Take no heed of my foolishness! I shall endeavour not to repeat this!"

She put an arm about the vicar's daughter and they descended the stairs together, whispering and giggling like children, so that the small excursion from their rooms took on the flavour of an adventure. Louise could not forget the vivid dream, but she was grateful for Milly's well-meant intervention. The younger girl had been her true friend from the very first and had never tried to stand upon ceremony, refusing from the onset to respond to 'Miss Millicent'. They were indeed close friends, but Louise had no intention of revealing the truth of her nightmare to Milly, for all that. Somehow she was convinced that the frightening dream was linked in some way with those elusive images seen earlier in her mirror. It was an odd, unsettling impression that would not easily be dismissed. Louise tossed wakefully in her bed for a full hour after she had bidden her friend a final good night.

When next morning dawned bright and sunny, the night's unpleasantness was set aside. It was not until Louise reached out to put on her locket, that a shudder of remembrance seized her. Thoughtfully and scarcely knowing why, she fastened the clasp of the locket, then allowed the ornament to slip into concealment beneath the neck of her gown. With an effort, she commenced her morning duties, setting tasks for the maids, before busying herself with the making of fruit pies from last summer's preserves. Eventually she recovered her habitual calm and peace of mind, for she revelled in the space and convenience of the vicarage kitchen. Granfer's small brick oven had given little scope for imaginative baking! She hummed a tune beneath her breath and smiled out of the window at a group of sparrows, squabbling noisily over a crust of bread. It was a very *small* crust, she thought humorously. Young Carrie must have heeded her words and decided to economise at the birds' expense!

The pies were in the oven and Louise was washing floury hands, when Millicent Parswell burst excitedly into the kitchen, her light blue eyes gleaming with interest and speculation.

"Louise — we have a *visitor*!" she said importantly. "I have put him into Papa's study. Would you go to him, please? I must find Papa!"

"A visitor?" echoed Louise, drying her hands thoughtfully and removing her enveloping apron. Her colour rose as she asked diffidently: "Is it someone from the Hall, Milly?"

"Oh, no!" said Millicent cheerfully. "Gerard and Piers are up in Yorkshire with their uncle and Sir Reginald is away on business. No — *he* has not come from the Hall!"

"Oh!" murmured Louise, vaguely

irritated by her friend's air of mystery. It was often difficult to assume a complete lack of interest in the Challis family — beyond admitting to normal gratitude. Rarely hearing news of the twin heirs, she never asked questions about them. Milly always seemed to know of their whereabouts, but a mere housekeeper must try to keep to her place!

The Challis heirs were now grand young men of twenty-four, thought Louise wistfully. It was highly unlikely that she would ever further her acquaintance with either of them. She reined in this line of thought, for Milly was hovering still at the kitchen door.

"It is a *man*," said the vicar's daughter, rolling her eyes naughtily. "He is quite young and dark and handsome, but he is dramatically shabby and I sense something *mysterious* about him!"

Feeling vexed with trustful Milly, Louise hastened to meet the visitor before he should decide to remove himself — and possibly something of value — from the vicar's study. She paused at the door to pat her dark hair into place, hoping Millicent's father would soon arrive to deal with the stranger.

The man was of medium height and she saw only his back view as she entered the study. He appeared to be gazing out pensively into the garden through the window. He wore a less than wealthy air, as Milly had noticed, for his coat was shiny at the elbows. Louise's housewifely eyes took in the fact that his shirt collar had been turned to prolong that garment's life, but she was relieved to find him passably respectable in appearance.

She gave a soft cough to warn him of her presence and he turned quickly to face her. He was indeed good-looking as Millicent had described, as dark in fact, as the Challis twins, yet lacking their height and breadth of shoulder. He quirked up an enquiring eyebrow beneath her close scrutiny.

"*Madame — M'selle?*" he said, with a swift glance at the ringless state of her hands. "I am here to seek employment. The young lady bade me wait for *M'sieur le curé.*"

All colour drained from Louise's cheeks as she looked at him properly. She swayed a little on her feet, telling herself all the while that she was being foolish beyond reason. Those faces in her mirror yesterday had been but figments of her imagination, had they not? She must not begin to see those fancied looks on every newcomer who crossed her path!

"Ah — you are ill — no?" queried the young man in some concern. "You will sit here and I will fetch *M'sieur le curé* — no?"

"No!" said Louise hastily. "No! I am perfectly well, I assure you, sir! For a moment I thought — but, no, you are French, are you not, sir?"

His eyes narrowed and he moved so that he was but a pace from her.

"Who are you, *M'selle?*" he asked.

His tone was polite, but his eyes were cold and suddenly watchful. "I seek to be employed as tutor in this district. My references are of the best and I think *M'sieur le curé* will help me. You are — ?"

Louise had recovered her composure, but the uncanny likeness of this stranger with her mirrored images, made her uncertain. She could have set him at ease by conversing in his own tongue, for she had become fluent in the language. Yet, instinctively, she refrained from admitting knowledge of French.

"I am employed here," she said slowly. "I attend to domestic matters, sir. The vicar's daughter is but fifteen years old and does not yet keep house for her father. That is my duty."

The young man fell back a step, his eyes narrowing still further.

"You, too, are very young for this responsibility, *M'selle*?" he protested and there seemed more than common gallantry in this observation. He gave a brief, humourless smile, then spread his hands. "A housekeeper is old and ugly, I think!"

Louise acknowledged the insincere compliment by inclining her head but she did not return his smile.

"I will stay with you until the vicar arrives, sir," she said composedly, "but I doubt you will find employment as a French tutor in our part of Devon."

"The French are still held in dislike?" he suggested. "But this so-foolish war is at an end! *Eh bien*, I was *émigré* before this time."

She responded with a polite nod.

"The young lady, she has but fifteen years?" pursued the visitor. He added obscurely: "But she is fair. You, *M'selle*, are darker even than I. I think, perhaps, your age is more than sixteen?"

"I am almost eighteen," agreed Louise coolly, "although I am sure this cannot be of interest to you, sir."

"*Elle est plus blonde et vous êtes plus âgée,*" he murmured, as if to himself.

91

"Too fair and too old for *what*, sir?" demanded Louise incautiously.

"Ce n'est rien!" he said lightly. "So you speak my tongue, *M'selle*? I am glad the wars did not prevent the English from learning my gracious language."

Louise was both puzzled and uneasy at his manner and she was glad when Mr. Parswell entered the room. Thoughtfully she went in search of Milly.

"Millicent Parswell!" she said. "The stranger could have been a common thief and you left him alone in your father's room!"

"Surely he did not look like a thief to you?" protested Milly. "Did you not find him handsome? He is a little old for *me*, I admit, but you — "

"Milly — the man is French," interrupted Louise. "Yes, I know the war is over and we are at peace now with France but *I* would not trust this man with anything of value. His looks are passable, I suppose, but I do not like those near-set, calculating kind of eyes."

"I was not exactly thinking of *eloping* with him!" smiled Milly. "Ah, Louise — did you ever hear the tale of Sir Reginald Challis and his first love?"

"I think you are changing the subject, Milly!" suggested Louise.

"Oh, no, I am not," said Milly soberly. "Joking of eloping with a Frenchman set the old story in my mind. You have not heard it, then? Well — poor Sir Reginald was to wed this lady-love of his, but she ran off with a Frenchman on the eve of the wedding — well, *almost* on the eve, I think! Have you never seen the sadness in Sir Reginald's eyes?"

Louise hugged her arms about herself as if she were suddenly cold and she stared wide-eyed at the younger girl.

"Oh, Louise, you are shivering!" accused Milly. "Perhaps you have taken a chill? I had forgotten your upset of last night. Come — the maids are busy upstairs, so I will take my turn at making a comforting drink!"

Louise sipped the hot tea thoughtfully and was glad when Milly rose to her feet to watch the visitor's departure through the window.

"Our Frenchman has gone," she remarked. "If you are sure you do not need me, Louise, I will go to pump Papa for details!"

Left alone in the kitchen, Louise set down her tea and, with unsteady fingers, unfastened the locket from about her neck. Holding it in the palm of one hand, she looked down at it intently. The chased gold surface told her nothing and she wondered why instinct had caused her to wear the ornament beneath her gown today. She seemed to be developing an uncanny sixth sense, she acknowledged unhappily. In some disturbing way, yesterday's experience at the mirror, the nightmare, this gold locket and the arrival of the man who said he was a tutor, all seemed strangly linked as part of the same pattern. Her fingers closed tightly over the locket and she frowned.

The maids would return to the kitchen at any moment now and she could rely upon them to take the fruit pies from the oven. She needed to be alone!

I will go out into the garden, she thought. I will open up this locket and put an end to at least one part of my foolish fancy!

Her mind made up, Louise slipped out into the quiet of the vicarage garden, the locket held firmly in one hand. She paused when an evergreen bush shielded her from the house and looked down for a long moment at the locket, determined to open it, yet regretting that in doing so she might damage it beyond repair. Possibly there was a simple way of opening it correctly, she pondered, as she inserted her thumbnail into the hairswidth crack between the locket's two halves. She gave a soft sound of vexation as she chipped her thumbnail, but made no impression on the trinket.

"Perhaps I can assist you, Louise?" suggested a voice at her ear.

She started and spun round to face one of the Challis twins.

"But — you are in Yorkshire, sir!" she faltered ridiculously.

"We have just returned home," he said as gravely as if her words had not been impertinent. He bent and picked up something from beneath the evergreen bush. "I think you dropped this?"

Louise stared wide-eyed at the shining object on Mr. Challis' palm. The locket was now open! Mutely she held out shaking fingers to take the ornament from him. She attempted a laugh and held the locket tightly from his view.

"Oh — yes, thank you, sir!" she managed lightly. "How careless of me!"

"That is the locket from Caleb's cottage, is it not, Louise?" said the young man gravely. "Am I not to share its opening with you? After all, I was there at its discovery three years ago."

"Oh — then it is *you*, sir!" she breathed gladly. "I cannot tell you and your brother apart, you see. It is difficult to know whom I may trust! Please — what is your name? Which twin are you, sir?"

He smiled reassuringly.

"I thought we were friends, you and I, little Louise!" he said teasingly. "How lowering to find you do not know me from my brother! After all, we have met several times. You must know that I am Piers, the younger, unimportant twin! Gerard's hair is darker than mine and his eyes are lighter, but I doubt you've ever seen him properly."

"I believe I met him — once," she whispered, recalling that scornful kiss in the lane beyond the vicarage.

"Whenever *we* meet in future, I must announce my identity first of all," suggested Piers, watching the becoming flush rise in her cheeks. The little Vaughan was developing into a beautiful young girl, he thought, with an odd prick of anxiety. What was to become of her? Was it really *his* concern? Could it be that she had already met his careless-mannered brother? No one must ever cause pain to his little Louise. *His* Louise? He gave a mental frown, knowing it would be all too easy to confess to his deliberate avoidance of the girl. Was he afraid of the consequences of their relationship deepening beyond this present casual level? Did the sudden colour in her cheeks denote anything beyond natural embarrassment at their unexpected meeting? She was little more than a child, he protested inwardly. He set aside his troubled thoughts and indicated the golden ornament in her hand. "Shall we look inside the locket, Louise?" he asked gently.

On impulse she thrust it back at him.

"Please, sir," she murmured. "I know I am foolish and fearful, but would *you* look first and tell me what it contains? I have worn it about my neck for the past three years, but this is the first time it has been opened."

Piers Challis looked gravely down, then smiled at her.

"It contains two portraits in miniature," he said. "They are of a man and a woman. Can they have been your parents, Louise? You never really belonged in old Caleb's life, did you, child?"

Louise glanced down unwillingly at the small, delicately painted portraits in the locket's two open halves and her heart seemed to jump into her throat. The man, at least, was familiar! As she had half-expected and feared, he was the one she had last seen reflected as an image in her own mirror and *his* were the looks shared by today's French visitor to the vicarage. She was seized by an intensity of unexpected emotion and found herself unable to speak.

"You do remember these people, do you not, child?" urged Piers Challis. "Come, trust me! Confide in me if I can be of help. The woman in the portrait seems familiar to *me* also, which I find very odd!"

"I do not know her at all," murmured Louise, finding her voice at last.

She drew her eyes with difficulty from the portrait of the man. The woman pictured beside him wore a high-piled wig and an affected, simpering expression. Yet it was only the man's portrait that held her interest. "Sir," she went on. "A man called here today. *He* bore something of these looks."

She indicated the painted image again and told Piers Challis of the Frenchman's visit to the vicarage, the words beginning to tumble excitedly from her lips, as the conviction of some link between the visitor and her locket, grew within her.

"It is possible that the man in the portrait is your father, Louise?" asked Piers at length, seeming to dismiss the Frenchman as unimportant. "Now, think, my dear! You did not always live in Caleb Vaughan's cottage. Do you remember anything before your time with the old man?"

"I c — cannot remember," whispered Louise, her excitement ebbing and she began to weep. "Granfer said my parents died in an epidemic illness. I was ill too, but I recovered and came with him to Challiscombe." She dabbed at her eyes, surprised by her own show of emotion and added apologetically: "Forgive my foolish weakness, sir."

Piers Challis put out a hand to comfort her, but she backed from him.

"Surely you do not draw away from me in *fear*, child!" he said in tones of such evident distress, that her eyes widened, the tears forgotten.

"Fear *you*, Mr. Piers?" she said indignantly. "Of course I could never fear you. You have always been so kind to me — you above all others!"

"Kind?" he said with a wry grin. "Well, Louise, I must go now! I will come here again to see you, for we are friends now, you and I!"

This time she did not retreat, but shyly took his proffered hand in hers.

"Yes, you are my good friend, sir," she said softly, sure now that *he* had been the one to instigate her removal from his father's kitchen. "I owe you so much. But, sir — I beg that you will not speak to anyone of *this*," she added, swinging the now-closed locket on its golden chain. "Oh — I did not speak of that box you found with the locket that day. I opened it and found it to be empty."

"It held no clue to your mysterious past?" asked Piers, gently teasing. "Ah — but I had hoped it might contain a legacy in rubies, at the very least!"

"There is no mystery about my past, sir," said Louise hastily. "I am a very ordinary person!"

Piers Challis lifted her hand, which still remained in his. He put his lips to it in a brief, courtly gesture.

"I would never describe you as *ordinary*," he said, as he turned to go.

★   ★   ★

It was customary for the maidservants, Agnes and Carrie, to remain in charge of Sunday's midday meal, whilst the other inhabitants of the vicarage attended Challiscombe church. On the Sunday following Louise's meeting with Piers Challis, the church party returned to find Agnes in floods of tears and luncheon ruined.

"'Tis all my fault, Miss Louise," wept poor Agnes. "But I swear I never heard a *thing*! When I found the front door open, I rushed upstairs and found someone'd been up there thieving. I — I was so upset, an' that, I forgot to mind the meat an' vicar'll send me off wi'out a character."

Louise and Millicent soon discovered that only their bedrooms had been entered. A swift search proved that nothing had been taken, although Milly's bits and pieces of jewellery were scattered across her dressing-table, as if discarded by a discerning thief. The leathern box which had come from old Caleb Vaughan's cottage was open on the floor of Louise's room. As Milly humorously said, it was sometimes a good thing for one to possess little of value!

Louise soothed Agnes and promised that Mr. Parswell would not grumble at the change of luncheon-menu, in these unpleasant circumstances. Agnes and Carrie, supervised by Millicent, set the untidy rooms to rights and made up the beds with fresh linen to replace that which had been tossed on to the floor.

"It was probably just children from the village, up to mischief," said Louise dismissingly, although she did not subscribe to this simple explanation.

She was oddly glad that she still wore the golden locket hidden beneath her Sunday gown. Somehow, the locket seemed linked, not only with the visit of the Frenchman, but with this morning's furtive entry. Try as she might, she could not dismiss this startling, unfounded theory. She wished it was possible to confide her new supposition in Piers Challis, for he had called himself her friend and expressed a desire to help her. Yet, she could scarcely go to his home to seek him out and, even if she *did* venture to the Hall, she might find herself addressing Mr. Gerard by mistake!

Naturally enough, the indignant vicar reported the outrage to his patron, Sir Reginald, on his return home, but that gentleman held the view tentatively put forward by Louise. Of course, only mischievous children would find sport in breaking-in to the vicar's home, decided Sir Reginald bluffly. Nothing had been taken and the matter was best forgotten!

Yet Louise found difficulty in forgetting either Sunday's intruder or the Frenchman's visit. Although she resolved not to speak again of the former, the latter's disturbing likeness to the man's portrait in her locket, led her into a little discreet questioning of Mr. Parswell. As there was little scope for a tutor in foreign languages in the area, revealed the vicar, one could only surmise that the fellow had moved to another district in search of employment. With this unsatisfactory explanation, Louise attempted to dismiss the entire episode from her mind. Yet, she found herself thinking, with disquieting persistence that they had not seen the last of the dark stranger from France.

5

MAY day of that year of 1802 dawned bright and warm and the May revels took place, as usual, in the village of Challiscombe, beneath a cloudless sky. The maypole was erected on the village green in front of the inn and Raymond Beckwith and his wife did good trade from early morning to late evening.

Mr. Parswell, vicar of Challiscombe and district, welcomed any event which had become an historical tradition. History was his hobby and he chose to gloss over the fact that Maytime revels were of pagan origin. He smiled benignly when his maidservants, Carrie and Agnes, spoke of rising early to bathe their faces in May-dew and shook his head in mock vexation that they should expect a magical improvement of the looks bestowed upon them by the good Lord. May Day was harmless enough, said the vicar, if the festivities were kept within proper limits. He frowned upon the pairing up of young maids and men in the evening and urged parental supervision when dusk began to fall. Perhaps the revels were less unseemly here in Challiscombe, than were rumoured of other areas, yet the enjoyment culled from this occasion was equalled only by that of Harvest and Christmas.

Louise Vaughan was now eighteen years of age and judged herself too old and staid to indulge in Maytime frolics, but she allowed the vicar's daughter to persuade her to go into the village again in the early evening.

"Do say you will come!" pleaded the younger girl. "Papa will forbid my going alone but he will trust *you* to look after me!"

"You're learning wheedling ways, Milly!" laughed Louise. "But if your father permits the excursion, then I will be glad to go with you. After all, he does not condemn this anniversary and he even went with us to watch the maypole dancing today. Perhaps he will allow us to go to the village again, if we promise not to stay after dark. *That* would be unwise!"

Mr. Parswell had no objection to the plan and so the two girls walked into Challiscombe, knowing they might stay until the approach of the supper-hour. Agnes was to cook the meal. The maid was soon to wed a local fisherman and was eager for opportunities of practising her culinary skill.

The festivities were in full swing upon the village green when the girls arrived and Louise noted with a qualm of uneasiness that some of the revellers were already more than a little intoxicated. Belatedly she wondered if they had been wise to come here this evening.

"Stay by my side, Milly," she urged the younger girl firmly. "Some of the men have taken too much ale and might forget you are the vicar's daughter. They are not bad lads and they would be horrified if they found out later that they had insulted you, love!"

Millicent pulled a wry face and murmured naughtily that being a vicar's daughter had certain drawbacks, but she acknowledged the wisdom of keeping close to her friend. Annis Beckwith saw them approach the village green and beckoned them towards the side door of the inn.

"Come you in, young ladies," beamed the kindly wife of the inn-keeper. "See — I have Miss Millicent's favourite sweetmeats here!"

She offered the traditional May-fare of toffee stick biscuits and fruit cup in tall glasses, but Louise refused them with a smile.

"We had tea at the vicarage before we set out, Mrs. Beckwith," she said, then cast her friend a quizzical look. "I dare say *you* will be hungry again already, Milly?"

Young Miss Parswell nodded eagerly

and watched Annis Beckwith pour out her fruit cup. Louise shook her head in mock resignation at her friend's youthful appetite, then wandered out of the doorway, knowing that Milly was safe from insult beneath Mrs. Beckwith's care.

Louise ventured a few steps away from the inn, intending to play the part of spectator until the vicar's daughter had had a sufficiency of Maytime delicacies. Yet she did not draw back when her hands were seized by a laughing village youth, who stepped out of the throng of dancers to join her. She recognised him as a friend of Agnes's betrothed and allowed him to dance her round the green until they were both breathless. The boy left with a nod and a grin and she found that she was now standing beside the small bonfire, traditionally kindled on the first of May and kept burning from afternoon to evening.

For a moment, she stood alone beside the fire's glow, nodding her head in time to the lively tune of the trio of fiddlers, who had been playing almost non-stop since morning. Then, recalling the younger girl in her care, she turned to go back to the inn. Even as she moved from the bonfire, a figure detached itself from the shadows of early evening and came to stand beside her.

"Oh — it is *you*, Mr. Piers!" she said, recognising the man at her side. "I think I am still a child at heart, for I am thoroughly enjoying the dancing and the music."

Her gay smile faded when Mr. Challis took her arm urgently and led her away from the merriment. He drew her behind a sheltering chestnut tree and she shivered as the tree's bulk shielded her from the bonfire's warmth.

"Mr. Piers?" she said softly. "Is something wrong? I — "

Her words came to an abrupt halt when Mr. Challis grasped her firmly by the arms. For a startled moment she blinked dazedly up into his eyes, unable to read his expression in the shade of the tree. He smiled, then, without warning, lowered his head and held her captive in a kiss which robbed her of her breath. Her own response amazed her, for she found she was holding tightly to his coat, returning the embrace with unmaidenly fervency and wishing the moment could last for eternity. In the end, it was he and not she who drew away.

"Well, then!" remarked the young man musingly. "Now was that intended for brother Piers? Surely you can see I am *Gerard*? Come now, little Miss Vaughan — will you not kiss me again, for my *own* sake?"

Louise struggled away from his mocking gaze, her eyes wide with horrified realisation, then she scrubbed childishly at her betraying lips with the back of one hand. Of course, Piers Challis would not kiss her in this way! How could she have been so foolish as to suppose she meant anything at all to *him*? Worse than this even — she had allowed Mr. Gerard to guess at her feelings for his brother, a feeling not totally acknowledged until now, even to herself. She stared at the lazily smiling Gerard Challis and hated him suddenly for forcing her secret thoughts out into the open. Well — she would disappoint him! He was expecting her to burst into tears or to aim a blow at his mocking handsome face. Instead she would dismiss his embrace casually.

"Sir — you overwhelm me!" she said lightly, her voice pleasingly steady. "I vow I have been treated affectionately by a deal of men who will regret it on the morrow. Come, Mr. Challis — do not look so guilty, I beg you! After all, what is a mere kiss on May Day? Do not fear I will shame you before your family by asking for an apology when you are sober!"

With a swing of her second-best dark blue gown, she left him and made for the warmth and sanctuary of the inn. She was trembling violently and refused to dwell any further on the unpleasant and unsettling episode. She had little time to recover her composure before losing it again. The side door of the inn stood open and she could see that Milly Parswell and kindly Mrs. Beckwith were now in conversation with a fashionably dressed gentleman.

"Oh, Louise!" Milly greeted her eagerly. "See who has come to watch our May Day festivities. He has come into a fortune and need not be a tutor, after all!"

Louise stared incredulously at the Frenchman and her misgivings came flooding back. Yet could she still link this man with the newly-expensive air and well-cut coat, with the furtive entry into the vicarage some weeks ago? She must have been wrong about him! Yet he seemed to be watching her now with somewhat guarded interest, as if he sensed her doubts.

"Perhaps not a fortune, *M'selle*," he said, then bowed neatly from the waist. "I must introduce myself. I am André Durand and no longer penniless! I intend to stay here at the inn with the good Madame Beckwith." He nodded to the beaming Annis. "Perhaps I may call upon *Monsieur le curé* quite soon? He will rejoice in my good fortune."

Milly agreed quickly that Monsieur Durand must come to the vicarage again and Louise gave an inward frown. This André Durand had gained both confidence and conceit since his previous visit to Challiscombe, she mused. It seemed a matter of some urgency that Piers Challis should be told of the Frenchman's return. Her cheeks grew hot as she recalled her recent meeting with the elder Challis twin. If Piers should learn of that unfortunate incident, he would not wish to further her acquaintance — even to the extent of speculating on Durand's presence in the village. If only she had not mistaken Gerard Challis for his brother! If only she had not returned that embrace beside the chestnut tree! The thought of earning Piers Challis' contempt, even undeservedly, caused a hollowness in her heart. She set her personal anxieties to one side, took Millicent Parswell's arm and bade Monsieur Durand a lukewarm farewell. Swiftly she propelled the younger girl out of the inn, ignoring the many backward glances Milly was casting over her shoulder at the Frenchman.

"You are hurting my arm, Louise," said the younger girl in mild protest as they left the village behind and began to walk back to the vicarage.

Louise released her with an inattentive apology and Milly looked at her friend in puzzlement. Surely the young housekeeper could not have already formed a strong dislike of Monsieur Durand? *Something* was troubling her! Wisely the vicar's daughter held her tongue. Had she questioned further, she might have been rewarded by the dismaying sight of witnessing Louise Vaughan in tears.

★ ★ ★

Louise had no opportunity of speaking with Piers Challis until the end of May and by that time André Durand had established himself in Challiscombe as a man of moderate wealth, with an interest in history and architecture. The village folk accepted him as an eccentric and did not object to his nationality as long as the inn and the village store received his trade. After all, Frenchies were much the same as us, it was argued. It was not as if we were at war with France any longer!

Mr. Parswell and his daughter Millicent took to the Frenchman instantly, the vicar for his professed interest in history, Milly for her own reasons. Their approval seemed to set the seal on the newcomer's acceptance into village life. Only Louise Vaughan held aloof from him and he, in his turn, seemed ill-at-ease and wary in her presence.

Louise had been reluctant to seek out Piers Challis, in case she should find herself confronted by his brother and,

118

as the days went by, her sense of urgency became less. Lost in private thought about the Challis twins, she sometimes wondered gloomily if she had responded to Mr. Gerard's kiss because she had been attracted by some quality in the elder twin which was lacking in his more gentlemanly brother.

When Piers came again to the vicarage garden, she was aware of nothing different in his attitude towards her. So great was her relief, that she stumbled eagerly into speech about the Frenchman, Durand. Piers listened to her thoughtfully, having noticed both the initial wariness and the relief in her usually level blue eyes. There was more than André Durand upon her mind, he thought, wishing she would confide in him.

"I agree that this Frenchman *seems*, by all accounts, to be an excellent fellow," said Piers, "but I find it difficult to dismiss his likeness to the man in your pocket, Louise. Durand — if that is his true name — must have a *reason* for gracing Challiscombe with his presence! There is nothing of the penniless tutor about him now, is there?"

"I am still convinced that it was he who searched the vicarage several weeks ago," ventured Louise. "Perhaps I am prejudiced against him, sir."

"I do not see him as a common thief — and you are not to call me 'sir'," said Piers, his tone of voice unaltered, so that Louise blinked up at him for a moment, thinking she had misheard. "What would he have expected to find in the vicarage?"

"Why, *this*, of course!" said Louise positively, as she pulled at the chain to bring out the golden locket from its concealment beneath her high-necked gown. "He — the intruder — left Milly's jewellery scattered, as if he had searched through it. He also left my box upon the floor and *it* has the appearance of a jewel-casket, for all that it is empty! Yes — I am sure he was looking for an item of jewellery.

Durand has never seen this locket about my neck for I — I have wore it hidden since before he first arrived in this district. I am convinced that *he* was our intruder and that my locket was the sole object sought by him."

"Instinct warned you to conceal the locket, I suppose?" asked Piers musingly. "No — do not stare at me so, Louise! I am quite serious and do believe in instinctive reaction. This locket troubled you more than you would admit, although you cannot identify the people inside. Instinct tells *me* that the locket holds some clue to your forgotten past. Yet why should André Durand, a Frenchman, be interested in the past history of the grandchild of an old Devonshire beachcomber?"

"But, sir — Mr. Piers," she substituted, when he frowned at her. "How can I make you believe there is no mystery attached to my past? I am simply Louise Vaughan and old Caleb *was* my grandfather! But you are right about Durand's interest. When he first came to the vicarage — supposedly in search of employment — he spoke oddly of the relative ages of Milly and I. He said something about my being too old and Milly's being too fair. He would not explain his meaning. Oh, Mr. Piers — I am so troubled by all of this!"

Piers put a comforting hand upon her shoulder, to withdraw it hastily when a mocking voice interrupted their conversation.

"So you have discovered my little Louise, have you, brother?" asked Gerard Challis.

Louise paled and dropped the locket back beneath the neck of her gown, before turning towards the elder Challis twin. Her heart fluttered nervously as she anticipated a reference to that ill-fated meeting of May Day's evening. A quick glance at Piers showed a thunderous expression on his normally even-tempered face and she hated Gerard for his power to destroy her developing relationship with his brother. Surely the elder twin would not be so ungentlemanly as to speak of that unfortunate embrace? Quickly she began to speak.

"Oh," she said, her voice unnaturally stiff, even to her own ears. "Oh, this is the first time I have seen the two of you together, sirs! I think Mr. G — Gerard has the darker looks. How interesting it must be, to have someone resemble your own looks so closely! It must be very *inconvenient* on occasions, I imagine!" She backed towards the vicarage as she spoke. "I must go back to my duties now. Mr. Parswell will wonder at my absence!"

Louise lifted her skirts and ran for the sanctuary of the kitchen, leaving the Challis twins facing each other in less than amicable silence. Piers spoke first.

"She told me she had met you, Gerry," he said coolly. "What is your interest in her?"

"Oh — merely a passing fancy," said

Gerard lightly. "Of course, I see you feel you have a claim, brother! She is quite a decorative female — for one of her class, is she not?" He laughed when he saw Piers clench his hands against his sides. "Now, do not feel ready to call me out, twin! I'd not compromise a lass who is protected by — " he paused, gave a teasing friendly grin and added: "by our good vicar!"

Piers scowled inwardly, wondering why he should find difficulty in repressing an urge to begin a schoolboy brawl with his mocking brother. Gerry was merely using Louise Vaughan as an opportunity of goading him into losing his temper! The Challis twins walked home to the Hall in a comradely, if guarded manner, Piers brooding unhappily on Gerard's hinted interest in Louise. The elder twin had always been the acknowledged Challis heir, a fact which had never invoked envy in the easy-going Piers. Indeed, Gerard's gayer manner had taken him headlong into trouble since the early days of childhood. Piers sighed, wondering if Louise found him dull and unimaginative beside his livelier brother. Gerry would have confronted André Durand immediately on her voicing suspicion that the Frenchman had entered the vicarage secretly. Yet, Louise had not chosen to confide in Gerry, had she? She had seemed, if anything, unhappy in the presence of the elder twin.

Gerard Challis had taken only momentary interest in the pastime of teasing his brother about the Vaughan girl and, as they entered the Hall, had already forgotten the scene in the vicarage garden. The elder twin was beset by problems of his own making — problems which over-shadowed all else at this moment. Unknown to Piers, he had been gambling heavily in the nearest town and was not, at present, to be envied by anyone. Their father, Sir Reginald, was a man of substance and fair generosity but was *not* to be approached for renewal of funds before the sum set as monthly allowance was deemed due. Gerard had discovered this fact several years ago, when he had overspent his allowance to a very minor degree. *Then* he had been obliged to pass a mere week with empty pockets, but *now* the position was more serious. Instead of baiting old stick-in-the-mud Piers about the little Vaughan chit, I should be dreaming up ways of raising the necessary amount of cash to settle my debts of so-called honour, thought Gerard wryly. It seemed curious that he and staid old Piers should be twins, he mused next. Even in his mood of self-preoccupation, he had to acknowledge Piers' interest in the vicar's little housekeeper. Poor old Piers, he thought mockingly. His brother's code of behaviour would force him into playing the gentleman and forbid the enchanting discovery that the Vaughan girl was his for the taking! That enlightening moment on May Day's evening had revealed her feeling for Piers. The silly female had been frightened out of her wits that he,

Gerard, would speak of it today! Piers was a fool not to take the relationship beyond sedate friendship! Yet, for all his derision of his brother, Gerard Challis found Piers good for a small monetary loan that evening.

As the days went by, Gerard became desperate for speedy means of settling his pressing debt. Unwisely he had visited the neighbouring town and, by sheerest ill-luck, had met a man with whom he stood in debt to the tune of ten guineas. The sum was a mere nothing, thought Gerard angrily, yet in his low state of finances it was as far out of reach as a king's ransom! Small debts had a horrid habit of mounting up, little by little, into larger ones. Rather than approach his brother once more, Gerard toyed with the idea of speaking to his father. But he knew that Father would cross-question like a highcourt judge before he would part with a penny until allowance-day was nigh. Today's foolish journey into town had resulted in the meeting with yet one more minor creditor and Gerard's mood darkened as he rode homewards across the moor. Why — the fellow threatened *violence* if the paltry sum of ten guineas was not quickly forthcoming!

Gerard Challis, lost in thought, was riding carelessly and took an unlucky tumble from his mare, who chose that moment to start skittishly at the sight of a rabbit. It was, thought Gerard savagely, completely in keeping with the day's run of luck, that his being unseated should have an interested spectator! Another rider was upon the moor and had witnessed his ignominious descent on to the newly-unfurling bracken.

"No — I am *not* in need of aid!" snapped Gerard angrily, as a well-dressed man of medium height dismounted and hastened to bend solicitiously over him. "Take your hands off my coat, my good fellow! I am perfectly capable of standing without your aid!"

"*Pardonnez-moi, m'sieur!*" apologised André Durand politely. "I thought perhaps you were injured."

Gerard Challis brushed himself down with a thoughtful hand then reached for the dangling rein of his repentant mare. Why — this was the Frenchie who had come to live in Challiscombe. The fellow had an air of wealth about him! It would be as well not to upset him by churlishness. It was possible that a foreigner might be good for a loan without possessing that regrettable English habit of demanding to what use the money would be set! Quickly, Gerard adopted a more conciliatory attitude and together the two men rode on in the direction of Challiscombe. Unknown to Gerard Challis, André Durand was also speculating on the possible use to which he might put this timely meeting upon the Devonshire moors.

★ ★ ★

When his brother rode off earlier that day, Piers Challis went to the vicarage, determined to see Louise again. This time, Gerard would not be there to interrupt. After a moment's thought, Piers rang the bell at the front door and was greeted by the vicar himself. His friendship with Louise was not a clandestine arrangement, argued Piers. It was time that he acknowledged an interest in her.

"Ah!" said Mr. Parswell benignly. "I am just on my way for a game of chess with your father, young sir! Now — is it Gerard or Piers? I'm too old to start learning the trick of telling the pair of you apart!"

Wryly Piers introduced himself — a necessity on his every meeting with the vicar. It seemed that Mr. Parswell was determined not to distinguish a difference between the twins. The vicar went back into the house with the visitor and nodded when Piers stated the reason for his call.

"Louise? Ha — hum!" said Mr.

Parswell jovially. "Yes! I will go and bring her to the drawing-room myself! She is a fine young woman, my boy, and it is a pity she sees so little of people of her own age. Don't be misled by what she calls her station in life. *I* know a lady when I meet one!"

The vicar waited, obviously hoping for enlightment on the purpose of this visit, but Piers merely nodded and allowed himself to be ushered into the drawing-room. Mr. Parswell reappeared with Louise, beamed at the pair of them and suggested that they should leave the door open 'for propriety' as *he* was late for his game of chess and was sure that chaperonage was not necessary anyway!

Left alone with Piers, Louise sat uncomfortably on the extreme edge of a stiff-backed chair, her eyes down-cast. She looked up quickly when Piers gave a heavy sigh and was heartened to find that he was smiling down at her.

"I am so glad to see you, Mr. Piers,"

she began a trifle breathlessly. "When Mr. Parswell told me you had come here to see me, I thought he must be mistaken. I — I am an employee here — "

Piers frowned.

"I feel you are about to call me 'sir', and it will not do!" he remarked unexpectedly. He sat down upon a footstool, leaving only a small distance between them. "Let us first dispose of any feeling of constraint!" he suggested, his tone teasing. "Come, we are good friends, you and I, Louise! Do not pretend to be shy of me, after declaring you are glad to see me!"

Her blue eyes widened and her colour rose, but she smiled in return and seemed to relax a little.

"I have remembered something," she went on. "I could not help but think at length of all you said about my past holding some kind of secret. When I was a child — when I first came to live with Granfer — I had a dream. I dreamed it many times and forgot about it when it ceased to trouble my sleep. Perhaps it would have remained forgotten, if you had not urged me think of the past."

Piers nodded, thinking that he had never before seen a girl of her striking looks who was so unaware of their impact. Small wonder brother Gerard had noticed her! Their Yorkshire cousins could not hold a candle to Louise for looks, yet two of them had already secured husbands. Only Cousin Marianne was left at home with Uncle Thomas and she had planned out her own future. What did the future hold for Louise Vaughan? He suppressed a sigh. It was the *past* and not the future that interested Louise now and the fault of this lay in himself. He had been the one to bid her strain her memory for details of what had gone before her life in old Vaughan's cottage. He could scarcely grumble at the way in which she had obeyed him. It was too late now, to bid her forget the past and dwell only upon the present — even on the future!

"Yes, Louise?" prompted Piers gently. "What form did this dream take?"

"I dreamed I was in a boat," she confessed. "It was small and unseaworthy and I was both afraid and seasick. I was tossed alone upon the waves — no not exactly *alone*," she corrected with a shudder.

Piers took her unresisting hands in his and drew her to her feet.

"That was not a dream, love," he said, his grey eyes shadowed with compassion. "No — it was not a dream. You are speaking of the way in which you entered Caleb's life. You see, Louise, you came ashore in Challiscombe Bay and old Vaughan found your wrecked boat upon the rocks."

The girl stiffened but did not move from his grasp upon her hands.

"Why — why do you say this?" she whispered. "It is as if you knew it already."

Piers nodded.

"I escaped my tutor one morning," he said. "I had been watching the sunrise from the clifftop, when I saw old Caleb down on the beach. He waded out to the rocks and pulled in a wrecked boat. Moments later, there was a child with him. I was convinced that she — you came out of that wreck."

With an effort, Louise pulled her hands free and took a backward step.

"Then you have always suspected a puzzle in my background?" she said unsteadily. "Why did you hint and suggest, when all the time you were sure I was a — a nameless foundling rescued from the sea? You called yourself my friend and I — I believed you!"

"I was sure of nothing!!" contradicted Piers firmly. "I taxed the old man with my suspicion and told him what I had seen from the clifftop, but he fobbed me off with the tale that you and he were beachcombing together — that you discovered the boat together. I decided to let the matter rest, although I was far from satisfied with his explanation. I could see that he was afraid for you! Do not condemn my silence, Louise. I was a mere romantic boy, kept at home through ill-health and forced to study with a tutor. Your arrival in the Bay coincided with the height of the Terror in France's Revolution and I convinced myself that you were an aristocrat fleeing from pursuit. It seemed both exciting and daring that old Vaughan should shield you and claim you as his relative. Forgive my silence, love! I did what I thought was best!"

The repeated endearment brought a touch of colour to the girl's pale cheeks.

"But, *afterwards*," she pressed. "The Revolution is now past history. Why did you never speak of this when the threat of the guillotine was over? I — I find I do not believe your tale, Piers Challis! You have made it all up merely to present me with a — a romantic past!"

Piers faced her growing anger rue-fully.

"I have told you only what I saw that morning, Louise," he said quietly. "I may have imagined seeing the child appear from the wrecked boat, but I did not imagine Caleb Vaughan's gratitude at my silence on the subject. I recovered my health and was sent to school to join my twin. Wrongly or no — I held my tongue on what I thought I had seen. *That*, Louise, is the sole crime on which you must judge me! When I next saw you, you were a pretty Devonshire lass with a decided local accent. You seemed happy with the old man as your grandfather and he was transformed with his love for you. Why should a careless word from me, brand old Caleb Vaughan a liar and rob you both of happiness? Besides — I was no longer sure of what I had seen that morning. Would you have had me risk an old man's happiness for mere supposition?"

Louise found her own anger cooling

into alarm before the change in the normally calm Piers Challis. She took another backward step, only to be seized firmly in a bruising grip by the new, far from gentle, Piers.

"I — I am *not* judging you, sir," she protested.

"Do not call me 'sir'!" he grated in exasperation.

They stared breathlessly at each other for a long moment, then Piers drew her closer to him and kissed her, his anger spent. Louise leaned against him, her sole emotion one of relief.

"D — do not forget that the door is open," she said eventually.

He held her away from him, his hands on her shoulders. She saw some kind of inner conflict mirrored in his grey eyes and hoped, wistfully, that he would kiss her again. Instead, he released her, touched her cheek briefly with one caressing finger and smiled. He was master of his own emotions now. Louise found she was trembling and her hands rose to grip each other in a steadying gesture. If Piers Challis should begin to frame an apology, he would spoil for ever what promised to be her most cherished memory. Fortunately, he seemed to have no intention of apologising.

"Mr. Parswell left the door open for propriety's sake," he said musingly.

"Y — yes, sir! So he did!" agreed Louise with a small smile. "Shall I ring for refreshment, sir? Mr. Parswell would be annoyed with the poor hospitality I am showing you beneath his roof — "

She broke off with a squeak of alarm when Piers frowned, one hand upraised as if to strike her.

"If you persist in calling me 'sir', then I shall not be answerable for the consequences," he said, his voice deceptively mild. He raised a quizzical eyebrow and added thoughtfully: "You may tell our good vicar that I found no fault with the hospitality shown to me!"

A bright, becoming pink coloured

her cheeks and hastily she turned the subject.

"Do you still doubt that I am Caleb Vaughan's grandchild?" she asked. "Suppose the old man spoke the simple truth and you imagined the rest of it? If he and I *were* beachcombing together, when you saw us that morning, then it is likely that I am exactly who I think I am! Yes — I am sure that I am just *myself* and no mystery!"

"The dead man Caleb dragged out from the wrecked boat did not exist only in my imagination," said Piers levelly.

"A dead man? Oh, *no!*" breathed Louise unsteadily. "In the dream, I was never completely alone in that boat! There was a — a corpse beside me, but it was only a *dream*," she added in protest. "Oh, please — tell me that it was only a dream?"

"Caleb Vaughan pulled a lifeless man out from the wrecked boat," insisted Piers. "No, Louise, do not turn away from me! We must discover what really

140

happened that morning, love. It is too late now, to pretend that it never happened. You see, I believe that the boat left France with a man and a child aboard. Only the child survived the voyage. If — yes, *if* you were that child then who was the man? He was unquestionably dead. Louise — think well, love! Was the dead man your father? Was *he* the man pictured in your locket?"

"What purpose will be served if I *should* remember anything of the past?" queried the girl suddenly. "Oh, Piers — can we not let matters rest? Let the past keep its secrets, for they mean nothing to us now!"

"Then what of André Durand?" said Piers, in his old gentle manner. "It was his coming which so disturbed you, child! Did you not tell me how you instinctively hid the locket from his eyes?"

"Durand!" she murmured. "Ah, yes — I had forgotten him!" She sat down suddenly on an oaken settle and her blue eyes filled with unshed tears. "I feel I am being less than truthful with you, Piers," she confessed in trembling tones. "Everything you have told me of that morning on the beach and of the dead man in the boat, seems oddly familiar to me. I find myself convinced — almost — that Granfer met me then for the first time and claimed me as his relative! B — but I do not wish to be a F — French aristocrat, Piers! André Durand is French and I disliked him on sight — or *feared* him, which is much the same thing, is it not?" The tears quivered on her lashes as she whispered: "I want to be English, as you are, Piers!"

He came to sit beside her and put an arm about her shaking shoulders.

"My witless probing has upset you, child," he said, with a frown of self-condemnation. "Come — let me see your locket just once more and then we'll put an end to this inquisition — for today, at least. Speaking of French aristocrats has put an odd idea into my head! Has anyone ever told you about Barbara Trevanny?"

"Barbara Trevanny?" she echoed, obediently pulling at the chain to bring out the locket from beneath the neck of her gown. "No — I am sure I have never heard that name before? Who is she?"

Piers bent his dark head over the open locket and his breath fanned her flushed cheeks. He was so close that Louise found herself suppressing an almost overpowering desire to brush his furrowed brow with her lips. Her colour deepened as she acknowledged the effect his nearness was having upon her. All too soon, he sighed and closed the locket.

"In the library at the Hall, is a portrait of Father's faithless lady-love," he explained. "Ah — so you have heard something of that old scandal, after all? Barbara Trevanny was to have wed our father, but she eloped with a French aristocrat and still hangs in the library in disgrace, face to the wall. As boys,

Gerard and I sometimes turned her portrait to the light and congratulated ourselves that *she* had not been our mother! Louise — impossible though it might seem, the miniature painting in your locket is a little like faithless Barbara! I cannot be certain until I compare the two paintings but if this should be so, then this whole business takes on an even more intriguing air! You told me that André Durand reminded you of the *man* in the locket and if Barbara Trevanny's portrait matches up with that of the *woman* — why, perhaps we are already halfway on the path to discovering the locket's secret?"

Louise rose to her feet and drew in a deep, steadying breath.

"I have never been inside the library of your home, Piers," she said quietly. "Would it be possible for me to be present when you compare the two portraits? I — I would like to see the faithless Barbara who hides her face to the wall. Perhaps Granfer really

144

intended that locket for *you*, Piers? If he had recognised Barbara Trevanny's picture inside it, he might have thought the locket should belong to your family and not," she went on in a small voice, "and not to me, at all. In all likelihood, this locket was never mine! No — do not touch me, sir! Remember I was once just a lowly kitchen-maid in your home!"

"So, I am to be 'sir' again?" demanded Piers, then relented when he saw that Louise was restraining her tears with difficulty. "Come — I will tease you no longer — "

At this point, Millicent Parswell entered the room, a smile of welcome upon her face.

"Piers!" she said. "I met Papa at the Hall and he said that you were here. Why, Louise — you have not provided refreshments for your guest!" she chided. "I will ring for Carrie. I cannot *think* what you have been about, to be so remiss, Louise!"

"Oh, I have received quite adequate

hospitality, Milly!" Piers assured her blandly. "Miss Vaughan has looked after me, in your absence!"

Louise uttered a sound mid-way between laughter and tears and she escaped from the room, murmuring that she must repair her omission and fetch in refreshment personally.

"Really, Piers!" protested Millicent, when her friend had gone. "I cannot see why you must be so *formal* with Louise! I am sure you know her well enough to use her first name, as I do."

"Yes, Milly," said Piers Challis meekly.

6

"YOU'RE sure you do not want more of me for fifteen guineas, Durand?" asked Gerard Challis suspiciously, as he looked at the coins in front of him on the inn table. "If you really think this Vaughan girl is your long-lost relative, then why ask for *my* help? It would be easier on your pocket to go to her direct, instead of paying me to do your snooping."

The Frenchman suppressed rising anger with difficulty. Monsieur Challis wished for the guineas, that was all-apparent, but he had the Englishman's stupid code of honour — a code now foolishly at war with his greed for the gold!

"It would not be kind to raise her hopes," pointed out André Durand, with a shrug of his shoulders. "It is likely she is no more than an English peasant, after all. *My* young relative — if she still lives — belongs to an ancient French family of aristocratic blood. Only this child and I escaped Madame Guillotine! You must understand that there is no great legacy at stake — no legacy but our great family's heritage."

Fine words, my good fellow, thought Gerard Challis sceptically. If Durand were not so free with his gold, I would enjoy refusing to be his lackey! Yet, as matters stand, I am sitting here drinking brandy bought by him and preparing to sell him information. But, argued Gerard, no one could be the loser if he complied with the Frenchman's demand. If the Vaughan girl were indeed the fellow's long-lost relative, then he would be doing her a disservice if he *refused* his aid!

"Very well, I will do as you say," said Gerard finally, watching Durand's expression change from thwarted rage to relieved satisfaction. "Give me the fifteen guineas and explain how I am to earn it!"

"You are very wise, *m'sieur*," murmured André Durand, as he called for mine host to refill the brandy glasses.

"But I warn you," burst out Gerard, uneasily aware that he was setting himself in the Frenchman's power. "I warn you that our acquaintance will be at an end when I have earned your gold. Working for you smacks of spying, Durand — *if* that is your true name — and we English have long memories. Your country is the natural enemy of mine, for all that we are temporarily at peace!"

"Temporarily, *m'sieur*?" queried the Frenchman smoothly. "But, come — drink with me! War is for the politicians and the military! Surely we can be friends, you and I, even if we do not share a nationality?"

"You may be buying my services with your damned gold," grated Gerard, rising to his feet and slamming down his glass, leaving the brandy untouched, "but I'll be hanged if I'll have you claim my friendship!"

Mr. Challis marched out of the inn, glad that this meeting had been arranged in a place far distant from Challiscombe. André Durand seemed unperturbed that his companion had left without hearing out his plan to the full. The Frenchman rocked his chair back on two legs and hooked his thumbs into his elegant waistcoat, his whole attitude speaking satisfaction. He waited several minutes after the exit of young Challis, then stood up in a leisurely manner, finished his brandy at a gulp and slapped down an extravagant tip, which mine host gathered up with hasty greed, bowing subserviently. Money brought all men to their knees, thought Durand cynically.

The Frenchman was far from feeling ruffled at Gerard Challis's outburst. On the contrary, he knew that he now held that young man firmly beneath his thumb. That fine cockerel would not wish his father, the high and mighty Sir

Reginald, to hear that he had taken French gold to settle his debts, thought Durand with satisfaction.

Gerard rode homewards, miserably aware of the position in which his decision had set him. He had taken the fellow's money and must now dance his tune! As he rode on, Gerard toyed with the idea of telling his twin brother, Piers, of his utter stupidity, but condemned this whim as mere weakness. Piers would not understand how anyone could gamble away more money than he possessed! *He* would never have allowed himself to get into this unenviable state! Gerard mistrusted the Frenchman's supposed honesty and was convinced that he held wider interests than the mere discovery of a missing relative. Why had he taken such pains to stress the lack of monetary heritage? There had been nothing philanthropic in the Frenchman's expression, in spite of his high-flown words! I am an utter fool to have become involved in his dubious affairs, owned Gerard unhappily. If gambling is to make me beholden to men of Durand's ilk, then I had best find a less dangerous pastime!

★　★　★

"Piers, can you recall the spring of 1793, when you were kept at home with a tutor to teach you?" asked Gerard Challis tentatively of his twin, one afternoon in June.

The brothers were together in the stables of Challis Hall, Piers grooming his black horse, Jasper, and Gerard making a pretence of brushing down his mare, Pandora. Gerard rarely came into the stables, so Piers knew that this carefully-worded query must be of more importance than his brother's light tone professed.

"H'mm? Oh, yes, I remember that spring," agreed Piers, fondling Jasper's ears in a way that made the wild-seeming creature quite ecstatic. "I was out of tune with my tutor and soon

152

convinced old Dr. Polgarth that I was well enough to join you at school, Gerry! You must recall the tales I told of the merry dance I led the poor fellow?"

"Was — was it when that old Caleb Vaughan took in his grandchild?" asked Gerard, carefully casual.

Piers's hands stilled on Jasper's ears.

"Yes," he said shortly. "It was about at that time, that Louise Vaughan came to live with her grandfather." He turned to face his brother, his grey eyes angry. "Louise is not your type of young female, Gerry," he began warningly. "Do as you wish when you are away from home, twin, but do not think to carry on any kind of — of *intrigue* upon our own doorstep! Steer clear of Louise or — "

"Or?" demanded Gerard mockingly. "Ah, yes! We must not forget that you saw her first! Can it be that little brother Piers is *jealous*?"

Piers saddled up Jasper in silence, a tell-tale tide of colour in his cheeks and

Gerard thought ruefully that he had lost the chance of speaking further of the Vaughan girl's advent into Challiscombe.

"Fancy a gallop over Coombe Moors, Gerry?" asked Piers at length. "Your brain is addled, twin! A good strong wind will blow away your silly notions!"

But Piers rode off alone and missed the sight of Gerard tossing down the grooming-brush and striding off purposefully towards the vicarage.

Millicent Parswell admitted the visitor and her eyes lit up with welcome.

"Gerard!" she said delightedly. "It seems ages since you deigned to come here!"

"You can always tell us apart, Piers and I, can you not, little Milly?" he asked her teasingly and she flushed and dropped her eyes from his.

Louise Vaughan, halting in the doorway of the drawing-room, saw them together in the hall and made a startling assessment. Milly loves this man, she thought. Little Millicent Parswell loves the careless, seemingly heartless Gerard Challis! On this occasion, at least, Louise was in no doubt of the visitor's identity. She set her lips firmly, wondering if Gerard were aware of the younger girl's feelings for him.

"Good afternoon, Mr. Gerard!" said Louise clearly. "Come, Milly, dear! Ring for Agnes to bring refreshment. Mr. Gerard does not call here often. We must not send him away without offering him tea!"

Obediently Milly rang the bell, but her eyes were puzzled and reproachful as she noted the tone of her friend's voice. Could it be that Louise did not *like* Gerard Challis?

Gerard gave a thoughtful inward nod. It was not impossible that Durand's idea was correct, after all. The Vaughan girl's manner held something today of the imperious aristocrat, did it not? Intense relief flowed within Gerard. Perhaps Durand had been sincere in his desire to restore his supposed relative to her true status in life! Perhaps his own fears and feelings of guilt were needless. Gerard made a firm resolve to question Louise Vaughan in a straightforward manner. He had had enough of devious dealings! Durand had not, after all, laid any particular stress upon secrecy in this matter, he argued with himself. Everyone would profit if the little Vaughan did indeed turn out to be of the French nobility! Durand would be pleased; the girl herself would be grateful; even correct old Piers would stand in his brother's debt, for setting his lady-love into a suitable status above her present lowly one!

Thus convinced of his own high intentions, Gerard Challis set about making himself pleasant to the two young ladies who offered him tea and cakes — an easy enough task, for he was a personable young man who had no difficulty in exerting charm when the occasion suited him. Milly was

156

flushed and happy in his presence and his mood of self-congratulation hid Louise's reserved manner from his eyes. He left the vicarage, after exchanging a greeting with the vicar, who was reading in his study.

"If you see Monsieur Durand," said Mr. Parswell amicably, "tell him to call upon me when he has a spare moment. I have just discovered an important historical detail in this book. It throws new light upon the ancient origins of Challiscombe Church. Young Durand is very keen on architecture and history. My new discovery will fascinate him! Be sure to pass on the message, Gerard — or is it Piers?" finished the vicar inevitably. "I never *can* tell the pair of you apart!"

Courteously Gerard agreed to speak to André Durand, if he should meet the Frenchman, but he was sure that the fellow's professed interest in Mr. Parswell's own hobby was nothing but an excuse to detain him in the district.

★ ★ ★

"Piers — they are the same person!" murmured Louise. "Your father's faithless Barbara and the lady in my locket are one and the same! But I am sure she is not my mother, for her image is scarcely familiar to me. If — as you suggested — the *man* in the locket is my father, then why should Barbara's miniature have been placed here?" She tapped the golden trinket with one finger, then looked back at the portrait Piers Challis had turned from the wall.

"Barbara Trevanny ran off with a French nobleman called Henri something-or-other," said Piers thoughtfully. "It was our old nurse who told Gerry and I the tale, years ago, when we plagued her for an explanation of the portrait condemned to face the wall. Father could tell us more, but he has always refused to speak of Barbara Trevanny."

"Could your mother have been happy — living in the shade of your father's first love?" asked Louise impulsively.

"I think she must have known she really came first in his affections," smiled Piers. "From what our nurse said, Father had liked to think of himself as heartbroken, but she said that he would have been bored inside a week if Barbara had married him! How our nurse disliked the lady! I think Father would have forgotten Barbara and had this portrait removed, but for one thing. When she ran off without a word, she omitted to return some valuable Challis jewels given to her by Father. It was only this omission which kept his interest and his hatred for her memory alive. Our nurse said the reversed portrait was put here in disgrace, as a reminder of that missing jewellery."

"But it is wrong to hate in this way," said Louise with a shiver. "Hatred can only destroy people, Piers!"

He touched her cheek with a gentle finger, then put an arm about her shoulders.

"Do not weep for foolish Barbara, my Lou!" he urged.

She started from him, her eyes wide and dark in the dimness of the library. Pier released her, thinking his affectionate manner had displeased her.

"You called me 'Lou'," she breathed. "That is the name Granfer always used and it seemed so familiarly *mine*! 'Louise' is the name I have learned to accept but — "

"Lou could also be an abbreviation for Héloise!" came a voice with sharp, triumphant intonation and Gerard Challis entered the library. "Ah — little Miss Vaughan," he went on. "Is it possible that your name is really Héloise-Marie?"

"You walk like a cat, Gerry!" accused Piers angrily. "Are you spying on us, twin? What is this new nonsense of yours?"

Gerard Challis' cheeks darkened to a flush, for the accusation reminded him that he was indeed playing the spy for the Frenchman, Durand. He opened his mouth to protest, but at that moment Louise gave a soft moan of distress and sank to the carpeted floor in a limp heap.

"Now see what you have done!" snapped Piers. "Don't just stand there gaping, Gerry! Fetch one of the maids in — no, better still, go and get Milly Parswell from the vicarage!"

Gerard found to his surprise that he was obeying his twin and he cursed himself for speaking the name of 'Héloise-Marie' at an inopportune moment. Who would have expected that the mere mention of that name would send the Vaughan girl swooning all over the library carpet? What had she been doing in the library, anyway? Even though brother Piers had put his arm about her, one would not have thought the *library* would be chosen as a lovers' meeting-place. Gerard quickened his step as he went in search of the sensible normality of Millicent Parswell.

Carefully, Piers gathered up Louise's

limp form and deposited her gently on a velvet-padded couch. He kneeled in helpless concern beside the couch and took one of the girl's hands in both of his.

"We should not have tried to rake up the past, love," he said softly. "What's past is past and the chance that you are other that all you appear, does not matter to *me* one jot — "

"A touching little scene, my boy!" came a sardonic voice from the open door of the library. "Gerard — you are of age to do as you please but do *not* bring your light o' loves under *my* roof."

"I'm not Gerry, Father," said Piers, rising slowly to his feet.

Sir Reginald Challis lost his thunderous frown and he approached the couch to peer down at the unconscious girl.

"So you are following your brother's poor example, are you, Piers?" he said heavily. "You disappoint me, my boy."

"No, Father," said Piers with a shake

of his head. "You have quite the wrong idea. Louise has swooned and Gerry has gone for help. Ah — she is coming to her senses."

Louise's dark-lashed eyes fluttered open and she tried to sit up.

"Ah — I know you now!" said Sir Reginald slowly. "You are the grandchild of that old reprobate, Caleb Vaughan. Um — yes, shouldn't speak ill of the dead, and all that! Parswell told me you studied well and were worthy of being educated. That was Piers' idea, as you are no doubt aware!"

He did not speak unkindly, but Louise rose swaying to her feet, her eyes distressed.

"I — I am sorry I fainted, sir," she whispered. "It was foolish of me. I should not be here in your home. I will go back to the vicarage immediately."

"You will leave when I bid you to do so!" said Sir Reginald calmly. "Piers — I am not as stupid as you might believe. Sit down, my boy — you too, Miss Vaughan. Ah, good!" he added dryly.

"Gerard and Millicent are joining us. Quite a social occasion we are having!"

Milly Parswell gasped as she entered the library with Gerard.

"Louise — you are the colour of a tallow candle!" she said unflatteringly. "What have they been doing to you, love?"

Only Sir Reginald seemed to find Milly's presumption amusing.

"Ring for refreshment, Millicent," he said. "We must do something to lighten this atmosphere of tension."

By mutual accord, the Challis twins locked glances and silently agreed to omit all mention of the name 'Héloise-Marie'. Piers began to give an edited account of the suspicion that Louise's origins were not quite as they seemed.

After a moment, Sir Reginald held up a hand to silence his younger son. He reached out and picked up the locket that Louise had dropped upon the couch.

"Yours, Miss Vaughan?" he asked unsmilingly. "It is gold and obviously

164

worth more than old Caleb earned in the whole of his unsavory career as a wrecker."

"Granfer is dead, sir," faltered Louise. "Please do not blacken his name! He was very good to me."

"I knew him when I was your age, child," said Sir Reginald calmly and unexpectedly. "He was a down-right rogue, but he never did me an ill turn."

"My locket, please," begged Louise, holding out a trembling hand.

"Do not be so impatient, young lady!" ordered Sir Reginald. "First I must look inside this trinket."

"But — Father — " began Piers hastily.

The master of Challis Hall flicked open the locket, with what seemed practised ease and he regarded it for a long moment before he looked up at Louise.

"I was not mistaken," he said heavily. "How come a grandchild of Caleb Vaughan by this bauble?" His eyes hardened with pain. "This was once a gift from me to the lady pictured inside."

"*Barbara Trevanny!*" stammered Louise in shaken tones and Milly reached to take her friend by the hand. "Sir — who is the man in the locket? Can you tell me? He — he is somehow familiar to me.

Sir Reginald shrugged.

"That was Barbara's handsome French count," he said with a hint of bitterness. "If *he* is familiar to you, young lady, then you had best take yourself out of my home. A friend of Comte Henri is no friend of mine!"

Milly Parswell gazed in stupefaction at the trembling Sir Reginald and Gerard Challis cast his father a look of mounting alarm. Only Piers seemed to notice Louise's death-like pallor. He moved towards a manservant who made a timely entrance with refreshment.

"Come, Louise," urged Piers, holding out a glass to the girl, who was as still as if carved from stone. "Sip this brandy slowly, love!"

He waited for the servant to leave the library, then said calmly:

"Father — Louise knows nothing of her past and berating her for something she cannot even remember will serve no useful purpose."

"Of course, you are right — as usual, Piers," agreed Sir Reginald dryly. "I apologise for that unwarranted outburst," he said courteously to Louise, who was sipping obediently at her brandy and had regained a little colour. "Whoever you are, child, you were not even born when Barbara Trevanny left England."

Louise set down her glass with a steadier hand and looked appealingly up at Piers for guidance. This did not go unnoticed by Milly Parswell and she drew in a sharp breath of excitement, speculating on the possibility of her friend's being romantically involved with the younger Challis twin.

Piers ushered Louise and Milly from the library and Gerard was left alone with his father, who raised his brows in fierce enquiry.

"Oh, no, Father!" Gerard hastened to say, with a certain degree of self-righteousness. "This is one unpleasant affair you cannot set at *my* door! Louise Vaughan and her mysterious background are the concern of brother Piers."

"Be that as it may!" retorted Sir Reginald Challis coldly. "I shall expect a fuller explanation when my sons decide to comply with my wishes!"

★ ★ ★

Louise had the nightmare again that night and this time, when she awoke in shivering terror, Millicent was not there to give comfort. Louise gripped the bedcoverings tightly, stared into the darkness and willed herself to recall the terrifying dream in detail.

She was a child again, her only garment a skimpy nightshirt, her feet cold and bare, as she concealed herself within a cupboard, one eye peering through a crack in the wood.

Louise wiped her perspiring palms on the sheet and sat up in bed. Her child-self had watched a lady hustled roughly out of the room by a group of poorly dressed men, wearing the tricolour upon their bonnets.

She rose from her bed and went across to the window to stare out into the purple-black of the night sky, trying to focus her full attention on the starry pinpricks of light in the velvet dark.

"I don't *want* to remember!" she whispered as she rested one hot cheek against the cool glass of the window-pane. "The lady in my dream bore the looks of Barbara Trevanny, Sir Reginald's lost love, but where do *I* fit into this hopeless maze? I just want to be plain and ordinary Louise Vaughan! I am afraid! I am *so* afraid! Oh, Piers — Piers!"

★   ★   ★

"I am not answerable to you, twin!" retorted Gerard Challis, as he prepared to mount his mare in the stableyard of Challis Hall.

His brother reached out to take the reins and his grey eyes were angry.

"Gerry," warned Piers. "Do not think to fob me off like this! When you spoke that name 'Héloise-Marie' yesterday, Louise Vaughan swooned with shock. You are in some way in league with André Durand — a fact you'll wish to conceal from Father, I don't doubt? Gerry — we are brothers, yet share little but the same date of birth. Come, will you not confide in me for once? Tell me what you know of Durand and this Héloise-Marie person and let me set Louise's mind at rest. She has done nothing to merit your dislike."

"You talk in riddles, Piers!" complained Gerard, twitching the reins from his brother's hand and beginning to mount. "M'sieur Durand is an acquaintance of mine. I'll admit that, but as for being in *league* with the fellow — " he paused and laughed, although the sound held a hollow note.

Piers Challis stared for a long moment at his brother's averted face, then sighed.

"Have it your own way, Gerry," he said at last, adding: "I take it you'll not quarrel with the notion of inviting Durand to dine with us one evening? After all, he is an *acquaintance* of yours."

The elder twin cast down a startled glance from the saddle of his mare.

"Durand? To dine *here*?" he echoed, then added inconsequentially, "but Father hates the French."

He rode off at this point, leaving Piers staring thoughtfully in his wake.

An invitation for the Frenchman to dine at Challis Hall did not materialise and, indeed, Piers had not been serious in the suggestion. When next the younger twin rode into Challiscombe, he found that André Durand had left the village inn.

"And wi'out paying his shot!" declared the innkeeper, Raymond Beckwith irefully.

"Oh, he'll be back!" prophesied his wife, Annis, comfortably. "He's taken no more than a change o' clothing, Mr. Challis. Raymond'll lock up the room and Mr. Durand will pay up when he returns. Probably went off on urgent family business, I daresay!"

To avoid further questioning by his brother, Gerard Challis left for Yorkshire that week. Uncle Thomas was ill of the influenza and it seemed right and proper that one of the twins should journey to take the reins of Challis Manor farm, until their relative was well again. Sir Reginald set no difficulty in the path of his elder son's leaving, but Piers anticipated that *he* would have to bear the brunt of Father's pursuit for truth. Louise Vaughan had not been near Challis Hall since her fainting fit, but Piers had learned through Millicent Parswell that she recovered from her indisposition.

"Well, Piers?" asked Sir Reginald inevitably, on the evening after Gerard's departure for Yorkshire. The master of Challis Hall held out the locket which Louise had left behind in her hurried departure. "Are you ready to speak, boy? How came the Vaughan child by this locket?"

"I can explain that," said Piers with a sigh. "No, Father — do not frown at me so! It frightened me as a child, if I remember."

Sir Reginald gave a snort and shook his head.

"For all your childish sickliness, you were never afraid of *anything*, my boy," he said, "and fearing *me* was not one of your habits!" Piers smiled and poured his father a further measure of brandy. "Trying to get me drunk now, are you?" demanded Sir Reginald, but his tone was milder and the customary twinkle was back in his eyes.

Piers spread his hands and gave a laughing shrug.

"How well you see through me,

Father!" he said lightly, then nodded. "Yes, I can tell you how Louise came by the locket. It is my belief that she was sent to gain sanctuary in England during the French Revolution. Caleb Vaughan claimed her as a beach-combing find! He hid this locket and an empty trinket-box in his cottage. I was with Louise when the old man died and I found his treasures hidden where his finger pointed."

"You feel strongly about this girl, my boy," Sir Reginald stated rather than asked. "Don't try to prove she is a French aristo just to make her worthy enough to be your wife. Remember, she worked here once as a servant."

"If my aim were marriage with Louise, then her status in life would be unimportant," said Piers with stiff coolness.

"Then you have a *different* aim?" asked his father with troubled eyes.

"I feel totally involved with this mystery!" confessed Piers. "I saw Caleb Vaughan discover Louise on the beach on one of my early morning jaunts, years ago when I was kept at home with a tutor. Gerard guessed I knew something of her background and he sensed that all was not as it seemed," he hesitated, then decided not to speak of his brother's possible involvement with the Frenchman Durand.

"Why must we say that this locket came ashore with the Vaughan child?" queried Sir Reginald. "Even if she *were* a refugee from France, we cannot be sure that old Vaughan came into possession of the locket through her."

"I've spent much thought on this, Father," agreed Piers wryly. "Caleb Vaughan was a beachcomber. He was once a wrecker. He could have hidden the locket years before he claimed Louise as his grandchild."

"But you do not believe he possessed the locket earlier?" pursued his father.

"I was with Louise Vaughan when she first saw the portraits inside it," admitted Piers. "She confesses to recognising the man instantly. She was firm that the woman was not her mother. She is *not* Barbara Trevanny's daughter, Father — if this thought has been worrying you."

Sir Reginald rose to his feet and moved towards the reversed picture of his lost love. Its frame was not ornate and it was far from heavy. The elderly man lifted it down and set it in a chair beside his son.

"I commissioned a well-known artist to paint this," he said quietly. "The Trevannys were not rich and my parents tried to keep me away from Barbara." He gave a heavy sigh and Piers waited, his eyes on the portrait in the chair. "It was customary for Challis heirs to wed wealthy females, my boy. Perhaps your brother will put an end to this custom? *I* did not end it, for all I was determined to do so. Barbara met a French nobleman — we were then at peace with France — who was visiting England. She could not have loved me, after all," he concluded, "for she eloped with Monsieur le Comte Henri du

Pont-Rachelle and left only scandalous gossip behind. The Trevannys were decent folk and they apologised on her behalf and then left the county."

"She did not return your betrothal gifts?" murmured Piers.

"She did not do so — even though I had given her family jewellery without my father's consent!" retorted Sir Reginald. "I was well rid of Barbara and I married your mother instead. It was a good exchange, my boy! I only wish your mother could have lived to see her twins grow to manhood. She would have been very proud of the pair of you!"

"What happened to Comte Henri in the Revolution?" asked Piers. "Did you ever have news of him — or of her?"

"I'd hoped to question that fellow, Durand," confessed the elderly man, "but it seems he has left the district. Perhaps I'd best let matters rest where they are, Piers. Barbara will be almost my age now and time will have spoiled her looks. But I will not turn her face back to the wall. The necessity for that seems to have gone! Put her back in her place, my boy, for she makes a pretty enough picture for our library wall. Your mother's portrait is the only one that will remain at my bedside, never fear!"

Piers put Barbara Trevanny gently back into position between two bookcases filled with dry-as-dust and neverread tomes. Then he turned to go.

"No — not so fast, my boy!" ordered his father. "I've still to hear more about the Vaughan child. Come, sit down again!"

"There is little more to tell," said Piers. Now was not the time to speak of André Durand's interest in Louise.

"H'mm!" nodded Sir Reginald. "There is something of the lady in that girl and I'm glad you had the sense to press me into having her educated."

Piers' colour rose slightly but he merely nodded.

"The vicar speaks highly of her as a housekeeper, Father," he said, after a moment's pause. He held out a hand and added: "May I give her back the locket? She prizes it as a keepsake from old Caleb."

Sir Reginald's fingers closed decisively over the trinket.

"If she wants it back, my boy, then tell her to come to me for it," he said. "I've a mind to speak to her again and this should be reason enough."

Piers went to his own room, reluctant to leave the locket in his father's possession, yet unable to see harm in Sir Reginald questioning Louise. He made a resolve to be present and strive for the gentlest of inquisitions. Louise must not suffer further pain!

7

IT had been a long, fine summer day, but the heat had grown steadily more oppressive and by early evening storm clouds gathered above the belt of trees visible from the house. The old woman was sitting in her customary position at the glass door, which opened on to a trim but small garden. Every evening she waited in this manner, her faded eyes searching eagerly for movement in the growing dusk.

"Come away now, m'dear, you'm chilled there an' there be a storm brewin'."

The old woman frowned and lifted a skeletal white hand to hush the anxious maidservant.

"Go about your tasks, girl," she ordered. "You know I must not move from here until it is dusk. She might come back tonight, you see, and she must not think me vexed with her. If I am not here to greet her, she will know she has lost my love."

The rosy-cheeked maid shook her head despairingly. Her poor mistress was indeed crazed, yearning after someone who was, like as not, dead and gone these many years past. The master did not say much, but the situation was obvious enough to those with eyes to see it. The maid sighed and made a pretence of tidying the already tidy room, not liking to leave her mistress alone at this, her worst time of day.

The old woman was crooning tunelessly beneath her breath now and her pathetically thin body rocked as if she soothed a child to sleep. The maid had never met the erring daughter who had wrecked the lives of these poor old folk, but she hated her from the bottom of her kindly Cornish heart.

A low rumble of thunder interrupted the girl's thoughts and she moved towards the glass door.

"Let me shut out the storm, m'dear," she said persuasively. "It be rainin' in and you be gettin' wet. I'll get a good warm drink an' sit you by the fire."

Unwillingly the old woman allowed the maid to shut out the thunderous spots of rain, but her hand was firmly upraised when the girl reached to draw the floor-length curtains.

"She is here! She has come at last, my naughty one!" said the old woman in trembling triumph, her white finger shaking as it pointed to the trees beyond the garden. "Go, girl! Tell your master that she is home!"

The maid stared obediently through a rain-spattered pane of glass and her heart thumped when she saw a movement in the trees. It cannot be *her* come home, she reasoned, and felt afraid for her mistress.

A shot rang out and the two women, one young, one old, started violently. Their eyes turned with one accord to gaze out again, when another shot split the stormy air.

"Oh! 'Tis only a thunder-flash, m'dear!" said the maid in relief.

She closed the curtains swiftly and ran to prepare a drink. Hot water always simmered on the kitchen hob and it took only minutes to prepare the old woman's favourite weak brew of tea. When the maid went back she found that her mistress was not alone.

"Oh, you'm back sir!" said the girl in relief. "'Tis a bad time for her, wi' the storm an' all — "

She fell silent, her eyes wide with question. Her master a gentleman in his mid-seventies, was holding a sporting-gun and his cheeks were ashen. He turned to face her and she almost dropped the tea when the gun pointed in her direction. To her relief the old man set the weapon down on a table.

"I've shot a poacher," he said quietly, then sank down into a chair with a moan. "I was after a rabbit for the pot and this man rose up from nowhere. I — I was afraid. I shot him again!"

The girl poured out tea and fussed around her elderly employers, listening to the words which tumbled from the old man's lips. The poacher was, it seemed, a finedressed gentleman and not a ragged thief. James, the man-servant had taken him up to the guest-room.

"James brought the poacher here, sir?" echoed the girl. "Then shall I go for Mr. Markham, sir?"

The old couple were tenants on the Markham estate and had the right to take an occasional rabbit for the table. Mr. Markham would be pleased to have a poacher apprehended, would he not?

Yet it seemed that everyone but the girl, Mary, and the manservant, James, were to be kept in ignorance of the injured 'poacher'. When Mary took a turn at caring for the deathly-pale man in the guest-room, she had to concede that he was indeed a gentleman. His brow was bandaged and James had removed gunshot from his leg. Mary feared for her old gentleman. What would Justice of the Peace, Mr. Markham, say if they had a corpse on their hands? If he were not really a poacher and he died, folk round here, reasoned Mary, would call her poor master, murderer. It was up to her to see that the injured man recovered! She would not speak of him to anyone and she would beg James hold his tongue too.

When André Durand regained consciousness, he discovered the identity of his host and admitted ruefully to himself that this was indeed poetic justice. He had come to Cornwall in search of Barbara Trevanny's relatives, only to be shot to pieces by her aged father! The situation held wry humour, he acknowledged and he began to ponder on how he might use it to his best advantage. In all likelihood, Barbara had communicated with her family at one time or other. Perhaps these old people held some clue to the possible whereabouts of Barbara's daughter?

Gerard Challis arrived home from Yorkshire at the end of August, with the good news that Uncle Thomas was now in good health.

"Anything to report of the — er — mystery, twin?" asked Gerard on greeting his brother. "How much have you told Father? Have you seen Durand recently?"

This last was worded too casually and Piers narrowed his grey eyes thoughtfully. He answered his twin's queries and found Gerard relieved by the fact of Durand's continued absence.

"Mrs. Beckwith is convinced he will return to pay his bill at the inn," went on Piers, "but Raymond is beginning to growl about auctioning off the Frenchman's belongings to settle the debt."

"André Durand left his things in the village?" said Gerard with a low whistle. "It's definitely odd, twin. I'd say he bargained on a short stay away and has been unavoidably detained. Are you sure you've not throttled the life out of him and hidden the corpse, Piers?" he teased. "I know you would do anything to shield your little Louise!"

"Gerry — you are an idiot," said his brother mildly. "I have had enough to do in your absence without wasting time and thought on Durand."

"But I think you will have spared the little Vaughan some of that precious time!" retorted Gerard shrewdly.

"There *is* a development you had best know," said Piers shortly. "Father likes the idea of Louise being the child of his lost Barbara and has even spoken of becoming her official guardian."

Gerard whistled again.

"Durand is looking for *his* lost relative," he said.

"Héloise-Marie?" asked Piers grimly.

"Yes," nodded Gerard, "and you must admit that the name meant something to the Vaughan girl! Suppose she is really Barbara's daughter and heiress to the Comte Henri What's-his-name's riches? Suppose Durand is also a claimant to the fortune? The plot thickens, twin! Yes — I admit that Durand asked for my help in finding his lost relative, but I've done no harm! After all, the Frenchman might really be sincere in wishing well for this Héloise-Marie girl. It wouldn't hurt Louise Vaughan to pretend she *is* the girl — even if she's not! Well — Durand wouldn't *hurt* anyone, would he? Louise could only gain by — "

Piers cast his brother a look of angry despair.

"Gerry," he said. "Have you forgotten the way in which old Caleb Vaughan was beaten to death? Someone killed the old man and searched his cottage — perhaps for proof of this missing girl's identity. Hasn't it occurred to you that Durand could have been the culprit? Why must you credit the fellow with the purest of motives? I suppose," he finished wearily, "I suppose he lent you money, Gerry?"

Gerard gave an uneasy shrug.

"You've hit the nail on its head,

twin," he admitted. "I was an idiot to get involved with him, but I've not exactly helped him — even though I said I'd watch the Vaughan girl for him. No — don't call me out, twin! When Durand returns, he'll find me less than co-operative, I promise you. I know when I've been a fool, so don't make an issue out of it!"

"If he is sure that Louise is really Héloise-Marie, then he will not be absent long," Piers said grimly. "Are you sure there is some form of legacy at stake, Gerry? Did Durand hint that the missing girl is an heiress? His motives for seeking her out after all these years cannot be merely altruistic! He must *need* her presence in some way."

Gerard nodded uneasily.

"He did say that Louise seemed older than his missing relative should be," he said suddenly. "Twin — he spoke of a girl of Milly Parswell's age — of someone a little younger than Louise. I cannot have set Milly in danger, surely?"

"Let's have done with surmising until André Durand returns," suggested Piers, suddenly weary. "If he intends harm to his Héloise-Marie, we are at least on our guard against him now."

Gerard Challis eyed his brother with unwilling respect and nodded.

"Very well, I'll be guided by you, twin," he said humbly.

Piers burst out laughing and slapped his brother on the back.

"Not so solemn, Gerry!" he begged. "Come, saddle up your mare and I'll race my Jasper against her. It's a fine bright day for a moorland ride!"

★　★　★

Nothing further was spoken of Sir Reginald's suggested guardianship of Louise Vaughan and Louise herself was totally opposed to the notion. She sighed to herself. Perhaps she was afraid of being set in the position of *sister* to the Challis twins! Anyway, she thought, I *know* that Barbara Trevanny was not my mother. I am sure of so much, at least!

Strain her reluctant memory as she might, no new facts would come to mind. Hearing Gerard Challis speak of 'Héloise-Marie' had caused a tumult in her heart and she was not entirely certain that the name had not once been hers. 'Héloise' could have several shortened forms, 'Lou' being but one of them. She wished futilely that old Granfer Caleb was still there to advise her. Only he had held the key to her past existence and he lay still and uncaring in Challiscombe churchyard. If he had kept a secret locked in his heart, then he had paid dearly for it. Someone had killed the old man and had searched his home — her home. What could anyone have hoped to have found there? Her hand crept up to her her throat, but the golden locket was no longer there to comfort her. Sir Reginald Challis had kept it and who could gainsay his claim? According to the master of Challis Hall, the locket had been one of his many gifts to the faithless Barbara Trevanny.

Louise thought then of the box which had been found with the locket. It was difficult to credit that anyone would send a child from war-torn France with an empty box. Surely the box had once contained papers or other means of identification? Had Caleb destroyed the contents of the box? Did I really come here from France during the Revolution, pondered Louise. Am I the one that Piers saw as a child, down upon the beach? Perhaps I am nothing but the old man's true grandchild, after all? Piers was never sure that he saw the child actually *in* the wrecked boat, was he?

Louise sighed again as she thought of the dead man Piers had seen Caleb bring ashore. She knew that Challiscombe churchyard held many victims of the sea — fisherfolk as well as strangers from unknown vessels. It was inevitable that this should be so. It was far too late now to set about identifying the man Caleb must have handed over for Christian burial all those years ago, although Louise had pored over the parish records with the permission of kindly Mr. Parswell. It seemed that the dead man on the beach that day in the spring of 1793 would remain a mystery for ever.

"But," murmured Louise aloud, "if I did not come from France in the boat with him, how else but through me did old Granfer Caleb obtain the locket — a locket given by Sir Reginald Challis to his Barbara and, presumably, taken to France by her. She *must* have had the locket with her in France, for she inserted the portrait of her husband, Comte Henri."

Louise paused, her thoughts veering unwillingly towards André Durand, the Frenchman who was uncannily like Comte Henri in looks. Had Durand been in Challiscombe on the day of Caleb Vaughan's death? The old man had used his dying breath to liken his killer to the man in the 'little picture'.

Was André Durand a murderer?

She went about her daily tasks, chatted with Millicent, grew more closely acquainted with Piers Challis and his father and yet there seemed to be a gap in her life. It seemed as if she were waiting, half-consciously, for something to happen. Although she was not eager to see Durand again, the Frenchman's prolonged absence was perturbing and served to deepen her feeling of uncertainty. Why did he not return, if his interest were held in Challiscombe? It was cheering, at least, to realise that dear Milly had not been swayed by Durand's looks, as she had at first feared. Little Milly Parswell had eyes only for Gerard Challis and she made no attempt to conceal her joy when he returned home from his stay in Yorkshire. Louise had little faith in Gerard's strength of character, but she much preferred to think of her friend admiring the elder Challis twin, rather than the Frenchman against whom she harboured so dreadful a suspicion.

The days went by and golden summer was replaced by autumn's colour. The first leaves fell from the chestnut trees in the grounds of Challis Hall and the air was cleaner, sharper, holding a hint of frost. Still André Durand did not come back to Challiscombe and Louise began to accept that she could not be his sought-for Héloïse-Marie. Yet this was a far from satisfying thought.

"The name is not unfamiliar to me," she mused. "But if it is not *my* name, then who *is* she and who — for that matter — am I?" She stared at herself in the mirror in her room. "Do I truly remember *anything*? Was it really the reflection of Comte Henri that replaced my own on that solitary occasion? Who was the woman I thought I saw that day? I know that she was not Barbara Trevanny."

Her spoken questions seemed to buzz like honeybees in the quiet of her room at the vicarage. She would have to accept her lot in life, she told herself firmly. Only unhappiness and discontent would result from yearning after the long-forgotten past. She had formed the habit of going to Mr. Parswell's church in the early evening and strove to take comfort from her solitary prayers in that ancient building. Regrettably, she felt more at home in the library of Challis Hall than in church. Sir Reginald had bidden her feel free to borrow his books and the titles held a wider span than the volumes of archeology and history possessed by the vicar. Up to now, Louise had not taken advantage of her permission to remove books and return them when read. Instead, she enjoyed browsing in the vastness of the Challis library. Sometimes Piers came to keep her company and suggested titles which might be of interest. Gradually the two young people of such different backgrounds began to form a firmer basis for lasting friendship than mere transitory attraction.

Occasionally Sir Reginald himself

would come into the library on the pretext of selecting reading-matter. Louise knew this to be an excuse for observing her in closer detail, but found in it no cause for worry or concern. In her eyes, Sir Reginald had the right to learn more about his protegée. Yet she was thankful that the subject of her officially becoming his ward was not raised again.

With Gerard's return from Yorkshire, Louise was prepared to make a change in the pattern of her visits to the Hall but, somehow, her presence in the library never coincided with his. She had never forgotten his early attitude towards her and was sure he would not accept her as an equal. Her social background was not important to the younger twin and she told herself that the opinion of the heir of Challis Hall did not matter in the least. If Sir Reginald ever did make good his resolve to become her guardian, she judged he would meet with stiff opposition from his elder son — an opposition she would whole-heartedly share. She had not the slightest wish to become Piers Challis' adoptive sister!

Now that Gerard was back at home, Milly Parswell occasionally came with Louise to the Hall, only to leave her friend on arrival. Milly never went into the library and Louise knew that the younger girl only came to catch a glimpse of her admired Gerard. A match between the elder twin and little Milly might meet with stern disapproval, thought Louise sadly, for it seemed the custom for Challis heirs to marry women of means. Poor Milly was practically penniless. Mr. Parswell relied entirely upon his patron and even his daughter's pin-money came from her father's meagre salary. Louise had to acknowledge that her own case was even more unenviable than her friend's. Piers might be only the second son, but he, also, must look higher than the dependant of a poor country vicar, when the time came for him to choose a marriage-partner. Louise's evening visits to the church became less frequent now, for she was guiltily aware that her prayers held less religious fervour, than a heartfelt plea that in some miraculous way she might gain sufficient status to be worthy of Piers Challis.

8

"THEN you are leaving us?" asked old Mr. Trevanny gravely. "We wish you well, my wife and I. You will receive your thanks in heaven, young sir," he continued fervently, "for my poor words cannot fully express my heartfelt gratitude. Your tidings were sad yet, through you, my dear wife has found strength to come to terms with the situation. She will no longer sit and wait hopelessly at the window. She knows now that our daughter is gone for ever."

André Durand was a hard, consciousless man, but old Trevanny's simple yet sincere thanks smote something within him he had thought forgotten.

"Why thank me, m'sieur, for news of poor Barbara's unpleasant end?" he asked wryly, then added brusquely and half-ashamedly: "Madame Trevanny is a gentle lady. If my ill tidings have brought her peace of mind, then I am content."

The old man's continued thanks flowed unheeded over Durand's head. In truth, he was far from content with the situation. He had come to this remote Cornish village to seek news of Comtesse Barbara's daughter. But the only child beloved of these old Trevannys was their own lost Barbara, their naughty girl who had so cruelly left them years ago. They did not speak of the young Héloise-Marie and it was evident that they were completely unaware that they had ever had a grandchild. The Frenchman's sojourn in Cornwall had done nothing but waste his time and had cost him a permanent limp in one leg. Had old Trevanny hinted that he knew of the existence of the elusive Héloise-Marie, then Durand would have had no qualms about making good use of the fellow's guilt in causing him lasting injury. Pressure could have been brought to bear upon the old man — who, even now, could scarcely believe he was to escape punishment for firing twice at the supposed 'poacher'. As matters stood — Durand lifted his shoulders in a shrug which served to emphasise his nationality.

"No more, *m'sieur*!" he begged with a smile that was almost sincere. "This," he tapped his leg, "was but an accident. Your good hospitality cancelled out my hurts some weeks ago."

Mr. Trevanny fell silent, fearing he had embarrassed the guest by his eulogy.

"Your horse will be glad to go home, sir," said the old man. "It was kind of Mr. Markham to stable him during your — your illness."

Durand cut short his farewells to the Trevannys and their servants. He was eager to return to Challiscombe. The sought-for Héloise-Marie would not be found in Cornwall and he had no further use for his elderly host.

The girls, Louise Vaughan and Millicent Parswell, held his full interest once more. Louise was the likelier one, yet her apparent age troubled him still. If Héloise-Marie still lived, she could possess something of the Vaughan girl's looks, but her age would be closer to that of Monsieur Parswell's daughter. It was possible, thought the Frenchman hopefully, that *Monsieur le curé* had taken in a foundling-child and only called her Millicent, in ignorance of her true name and background. Surely the so-good *curé* would have given a home to a poor lost child? Héloise-Marie just *had* to be one of these two girls!

Durand frowned as he urged his tired mount down a Devonshire lane. Soon he would be back in Challiscombe and must furnish a suitable excuse for his absence and injury. He hoped that *canaille* of an innkeeper had not meddled with his possessions.

He must decide, he pondered wearily. Louise Vaughan had the hazy background that a fleeing aristocrat might profess, but her age — her *age*, he thought angrily. Near-nineteen held greater maturity that near-seventeen and that Vaughan girl had nothing of the unfledged looks of a schoolroom miss! It irked him sorely to be obliged to admit that his lengthy investigations had profited him not one jot.

He rested his horse and stared idly down at a cove similar to Challiscombe Bay. It was very early and the air was hushed and still, with only a hint of colour on the horizon to suggest it was time for the sun to make its appearance. Durand was completely unaffected by the beauties of nature spread before him, but as his mount cropped wearily at a tuft of stunted, salty grass, something caught his attention.

Down on the arc of sand, left smooth and damp by the outgoing tide, were two men. It seemed that they had appeared out of the side of the cliff on the top of which the Frenchman was standing. Unaware of their silent watcher, the men were busily fetching out an assortment of bales and small kegs from a cave in the cliffside. Durand stroked his chin thoughtfully, in no doubt of what the scene below him portrayed. *Bien sûr*, these men were smugglers and were in the act of disposing of a cargo brought across from *la belle France.*

For an instant, André Durand experienced a pang of homesickness, only to forget this uncharacteristic weakness, in deciding how to set the sight of these smugglers to his best advantage. He edged cautiously from the clifftop and walked his horse quietly until he judged himself to be out of earshot of the men below. His handsome features bore a smile, but his nearset eyes were coldly calculating his next move.

* * *

"Your smugglers' bay sounds too far off to fall within *my* jurisdiction," said Sir

Reginald Challis regretfully. "But I could lodge an official complaint against those unknown men who attacked you."

"Oh, but — no!" protested André Durand hastily. He spread his hands and gave the familiar shrug. "Some weeks have gone by since the incident. I am recovered now, *m'sieur*, and the men will have fled. I shall not waste your time with useless enquiry!"

"You're to be permanently lame?" asked Sir Reginald gruffly. "What about your head, young sir? I see a healed scar there."

"*C'est rien!*" said the Frenchman carelessly. "I come merely to explain my absence. Monsieur Beckwith of the inn was about to complain to you that I had left my bill unpaid. He is happy now, *m'sieur*, for I gave him money and will continue there for some weeks."

Sir Reginald seemed pleased with this news.

"You must dine with us one evening,

Monsieur Durand," he invited. "Perhaps our Devonshire hospitality will compensate for your treatment at the hands of the ruffians who were my countrymen."

"They could not have been men of *Devon, m'sieur*," protested the Frenchman with flattering charm. "Here, I have met only kindness."

"H'mm, yes — well," muttered Sir Reginald, embarrassed. "Well — we will make it something of an occasion when you come to dine with us. Have you made friends in this neighbourhood? Whom do you suggest might join us?"

André Durand appeared to consider this query at great length.

"You are so very kind, *m'sieur*," he said finally with a pleasing show of diffidence. "Perhaps you will also invite the good *curé* and M'selle Parswell? Would it be *comme il faut* for M'selle Vaughan — if that is her name — to join us also?"

"Of course, Louise Vaughan shall be

invited to dine," said Sir Reginald. "After all, she is almost a part of the family now."

Durand choked on the brandy he was holding to his lips and was affably patted on the shoulders by his host.

"M'selle Vaughan — she is to wed one of your sons, *m'sieur*?" managed the Frenchman at last. "I had not thought — It is *convenable* that a servant should do so in England?"

"You go too fast, Durand!" protested the master of Challis Hall. "I meant no such thing! Not that young Louise is exactly a *servant*," he hastened to add.

"She is perhaps of good family, *m'sieur*?" asked Durand politely, his narrow-eyed gaze watchful. "You must forgive me, for I am not yet familiar with your English conventions."

Sir Reginald gave a smile which told the seething Frenchman nothing, then rang for a manservant to show out his guest.

"I will not forget the dinner-invitation," said the older man bluffly. "You will hear from me, sir!"

Durand bowed stiffly from the waist to conceal his frustration.

"Then this is but *au revoir, m'sieur,*" he said evenly.

When Sir Reginald Challis was alone, the smile left his face and he frowned thoughtfully. It went against all instinct to offer friendship to a Frenchie, but the fellow seemed harmless enough. It was a pity, mused the elderly gentleman, that I was unable to investigate that supposed attack upon him by smugglers. I have the feeling there was more to that affair than Durand saw fit to disclose!

* * *

The dinner-party was to take place in the second week of November. The affair would make unwelcome extra work for the Challis cook, thought Louise Vaughan, as she recalled her time of employ beneath that uncertain-tempered woman. She smiled and told herself that her position had improved greatly, even though she might never become aware of her true identity. Since taking up the reins of house-keeping at the vicarage, she had received payment from the vicar. The sum was only a nominal one, but she had hoarded it carefully until it became — in her eyes, at least — a veritable fortune. Millicent Parswell was also in the unusual position of feeling wealthy. She was now seventeen years old and had received modest sums of money as birthday gifts from both her father and his patron, Sir Reginald.

"We will go to town and purchase material for new gowns!" enthused Milly. "After all, Louise-love, it is not *every* day that we are invited to dine at the Hall and we will be the only ladies in the party! It is up to us to display our beauty to the fullest advantage!"

"You are a vain puss!" scolded Louise, her dark blue eyes brimful with the laughter that came more easily to her these days.

Milly was crestfallen.

"Don't you *want* a new gown, Louise?" she asked reproachfully, then laughed in her turn. "Oh — you are teasing me, love! Come, let us ask Papa to accompany us to town!"

Mr. Parswell professed himself willing to take his young ladies shopping and, at the last moment, the carriage was joined by the Challis twins. Milly was eager to speak to Gerard, mounted on his mare, but Louise had eyes only for Piers upon the skittishly prancing Jasper. For a second their glances locked and a trembling thrill ran through her. She dropped her eyes hastily, so that no one could read their tell-tale joy. When she looked up again, Piers was smiling understandingly in her direction and she beamed at him in return. What did it matter *who* saw the exchange of smiles on this suddenly exciting day?

The carriage, pulled by the staidest of animals, made slow and decorous progress across the rutted moorland road and the Challis twins rode sedately beside it, or galloped ahead for a time, as the mood seized them. The weather was kind that day and the heavy November fog that Mr. Parswell had feared, did not arrive to spoil the outing.

Milly shed her new-found seventeen-year-old dignity and was a giggling child again as the jolting progress tossed her on to the carriage-floor. Louise could scarcely contain her merriment as the vicar strove to maintain his own dignity by holding tightly on to the doorstrap with both hands.

Piers Challis gravely ushered the ladies before him into the coffee-parlour of the town's largest inn and the party took refreshment to prepare themselves for the ordeal of shopping for their requirements. Mr. Parswell was eager to wend his way to the dusty old bookshop, which would afford him at least a full hour of delightful browsing. Yet first he had to weigh within his mind the propriety of allowing his daughter and Miss Vaughan to be escorted from shop to shop by two undoubtedly personable young gentlemen. He spoke quietly of his dilemma to Piers, the more sober-seeming of Sir Reginald's offspring, and was assured that it was quite the thing these days for gentlemen to accompany young ladies in the broad daylight of a country town. The vicar was easily persuaded of the propriety of the plan and the party made its exit from the coffee-parlour. The innkeeper promised to care for the carriage-horses, Gerard's mare and black Jasper, so nothing remained but for Milly to bid her father an outwardly demure farewell.

The vicar's daughter set her hand in the crook of Louise's arm and the Challis twins followed at a suitable distance. Milly was flushed and excited and Louise had to whisper with amusement that it was simply not *done* to cast so many backward glances at their escort. Louise had a ladylike dignity which seemed inherent and both Gerard and Piers Challis noted her smiling control of the younger girl and wondered at her instinctive knowledge of correct behaviour.

Gerard hoped that she was, after all, the missing Héloise-Marie and that the fact could be turned to his advantage with the returned Frenchman. Piers found it less easy to assess his own thoughts and he preferred to glance into shop-windows and smile gently at the aspiring men of fashion in this countrified town.

The small procession halted when Milly gave a squeal of delight and nodded her head towards a shop displaying lengths of elegant fabrics. In all likelihood the materials would be hopelessly expensive, thought Louise wryly, but she quietly bade the gentlemen wait and accompanied her friend into the shop.

"Now — do not peep, Gerard and Piers!" said Milly irrepressibly across her shoulder. "We are going to surprise you at the dinner-party!"

Gerard grinned and Louise caught Piers' look of sympathy. She propelled the younger girl forcibly into the shop, then joined with her to sigh with delight at the vast choice of materials.

Louise soon purchased a length of fine blue muslin at a surprisingly reasonable cost, but Milly was less easily suited. She held the two shop-assistants at her imperious beck and call, shaking a disdainful head as each new bale of cloth was produced for her inspection. This procedure went on for so long that Louise, waiting patiently with her modest parcel of muslin, became convinced that they would soon all perish from suffocation beneath a mountain of material.

When the proprietor, a portly little man, with the sad eyes of a whipped spaniel, appeared, Milly thanked him sweetly for his trouble.

"You see, sir, I just cannot *decide*!" she confessed, all blue-eyed innocence.

Louise was feeling vexed by now and

bit back the urge to shake young Miss Mischief. Milly caught her friend's narrowed gaze and hastily asked for a length of muslin, similar to that bought by Louise, but in a soft shade of pink.

"If I had not witnessed that with my own eyes," began the older girl irefully, as they made their exit, leaving a welter of confusion behind them.

"Oh, pray do not scold me and spoil things!" begged Milly contritely. "It was such capital fun and I vow I've never enjoyed myself so much before in my *entire* life!"

Naturally enough, their waiting escorts demanded to be told the reason for this excess of merriment, for both of the girls were now helpless with laughter. When the amusement had abated, the young people began to walk four-abreast, chatting in a more relaxed manner. Laughter pealed forth again when a dandified man of uncertain age and tremendous girth observed that they were blocking the footpath.

The two ladies needed long gloves

and ribbons to decorate the gowns they planned to make and Gerard pretended to enter the haberdashers with them. It was Milly's turn to gasp at impropriety now. This so amused Piers that he had to turn away to dab tears of laughter from his eyes.

All merriment left him as his gaze was met by a shifty glance from an unsavoury-looking individual with a frayed muffler round his neck. The man ducked guiltily out of sight round a corner, verifying Piers' surmise that he had indeed been watching them. Suddenly Piers made up his mind that he had seen those same watching eyes earlier in the day and he sped in pursuit of the fleeing man.

Indignant ladies and gentlemen stepped aside as Piers weaved in and out of the window-gazing crowds. He lost his beaver top-hat in his haste and his coat-tails flapped and impeded his progress. It seemed strangely important that the watcher should not escape unquestioned.

It was a somewhat breathless Piers Challis who returned to the haberdasher's shop, hat in hand and a film of perspiration on his brow. He said little to his curious brother, but his burst of speed had been rewarded by a sight which gave odd clarification to the close observance of the party from Challiscombe. The man with the muffler had slipped into a small, unhygienic-looking tavern. Through its dirty windows, Piers had seen the subject of his pursuit in conversation with none other than the Frenchman, André Durand! Thoughtfully he had refrained from entering the tavern to demand an explanation.

The shopping-party went back to take further refreshment at the coffee-parlour and were joined there by a beaming Mr. Parswell, his hands lovingly caressing an ancient, dog-eared volume entitled: 'A Progress of Architecture'. Beyond querying the fact that Piers' beaver hat was trodden-on and past repair, no one but Louise noted any change in the demeanour of the younger Challis twin. On the homeward journey, only Gerard paused to pass occasional teasing comment through the carriage window. Piers rode ahead, almost as if he had forgotten the existence of his travelling-companions. Sadly Louise wondered if she had read too much into his earlier carefree attitude. Surely a ruined hat could not be to blame for Piers' sudden desire for his own company?

That evening, a heavy mist rolled in from the sea, to mingle with a growing density of November fog on land. Inside the vicarage, a haven of warmth against the onslaught of winter, Milly Parswell exclaimed anew over her purchases. She was mildly puzzled not to draw a reminiscent chuckle from Louise, when she referred to her naughtiness in causing such a confusion of fabrics in the shop. She was not to know that her friend was too much concerned with the seeming change in Piers Challis, to attend to her childish glee. Going to the kitchen in search of a hot posset, Milly decided that the horrid fog had given poor Louise the headache.

9

THE dinner-party was something of a success, but the young ladies were glad the time came to leave the gentlemen alone with their port.

Louise held out her hands to the welcome blaze of the drawing-room fire and Milly twitched her stool closer to the hearth with a shiver.

"We look elegant enough in our new gowns, Louise," said the younger girl pensively, as she lifted her hem to allow the warmth to reach her chilled ankles. "I suppose pride in one's appearance must always have a price."

"Yes," agreed Louise with a smile. "Summer-weight muslin is scarcely the thing to wear in November, love!"

"The fine London ladies might not wear much beneath *their* gowns," said Milly frankly, "but I am glad I put on my thick winter petticoat tonight!"

The arrival of coffee caused the older girl to hush her friend's innocent mention of undergarments, for the tray was carried by the awe-inspiring Wentworth himself. During her employment in the Challis kitchen, Louise had scarcely come into contact with the imposing butler, but she was sure he must disapprove to see her, a former servant, being treated as a welcome guest in his master's house.

The remaining coffee was becoming cool and the two girls sleepy with their proximity to the fire, when Piers Challis entered the drawing-room, a very serious expression upon his face. Drowsiness fell like a cloak from Louise and she rose to greet him. He paused by the branched candelabra on a side table and signalled her to join him quietly, so that they did not attract the attention of Milly who was almost asleep.

"Something is wrong!" guessed Louise in a taut whisper. "None of you came in for coffee and — "

Piers put a gentle finger to her lips and silenced her questions.

"There is some form of commotion in Challiscombe Bay," he said quietly. "Father and Gerard have ridden off to investigate."

"Monsieur Durand too?" interrupted Louise urgently. "Did he go with them or is he still with Mr. Parswell? Remember that he is a Frenchman and that any kind of *commotion* on our coast could herald a French invasion! Oh, Piers! Have the French attacked us?" Her eyes were wide and dark in the flickering light of the candles and she gripped her hands together to stay their trembling. "Why did *you* not go with your father, Piers?"

He touched her cheek fleetingly, distracted from the present situation by the picture of beauty Louise presented in her simple muslin gown, with her dark curls threaded by a blue ribbon which matched her gloves.

"Jasper lost a shoe and I was forced

223

to come back," he said lightly, noting the natural way her hand rose to take his. "This is no invasion, love, for we have been at peace with the French since the springtime Amiens Treaty. You know that Father is a Justice of the Peace. It is his normal duty to settle any kind of trouble with the local smugglers."

"*Smugglers?*" she echoed, clutching tightly at his hand. "Durand was supposed to be hurt by smugglers, was he not? But Piers — you did not tell me where *he* is now! Did he go with your father?"

"He saddled up his horse and rode off with Gerard," frowned Piers. "He'll not come to any harm."

Louise released his hand suddenly.

"I do not fear for *him*," she said and Milly moaned and stirred in her uneasy sleep beside the fire.

Piers cast the sleeping girl a quick glance, took Louise by her trembling shoulders and bent his head to kiss her lightly. She clung to him almost desperately, whispering aloud her distrust of the Frenchman.

"I fear him without proper reason," she said more composedly, her cheek against the starched ruffles of Piers' shirt.

He put her from him and lifted her chin with one finger, so that her blue eyes were obliged to meet his reassuring grey ones.

"If the local smugglers have chosen tonight to land a cargo, they will have the Customs' men to reckon with as well as Father and Gerard, do not fear! Durand can only be a spectator to whatever is happening down on the beach, love," he said comfortingly. "But, you are right! I should be there to keep an eye on matters. I do not trust the fellow myself. I have not yet found out why he employed someone to watch us — " He met Louise's anxious look and went on unwillingly to tell her about the man in the muffler who had spied upon them on the day of the shopping expedition. "But there is nothing to worry about, Louise," he said persuasively.

She slipped from his clasp and looked away. Her voice was low and unsteady.

"I have been thinking," she murmured, "that Durand would go away if I told him my name was — was Héloise-Marie. Perhaps I am truly his lost relative and am setting you all in danger by refusing to admit to it."

Piers took her hands again and gave them a gentle shake.

"André Durand is but one lone man in a strange country!" he chided. "Even if he wished harm to anyone here in England, he would find difficulty in implementing his threats. Louise," he commanded, "look at me, love — has he threatened *you* in any way?"

"No — oh, I do not know!" she said, tears sparkling in the candlelight on her long lashes. "His eyes are cruel, Piers! Every time I see those eyes, I know he is seeking vengeance."

"*Vengeance?*" said Piers lightly.

"Your imagination reads too much into the actions of that little Frenchman!"

Louise gave a watery smile.

"You call him little," she said. "It is all very well for you with your excessive height, Piers Challis!"

"Perhaps all Frenchmen are of meagre height," teased Piers to keep the smile upon her tear-wet cheeks. "They say Napoleon Bonaparte himself is only five and a half feet tall!"

Louise accepted a linen handkerchief from Piers and dabbed at her eyes, but she shivered suddenly.

"Bonaparte is a dangerous man!" she whispered. "His height does not matter. From all we hear, he is a *monster*!"

"Then do not believe all you hear, love," bade Piers solemnly.

Further talk was made impossible when Milly Parswell awoke and rose yawning from her seat by the fire. Her father, the vicar, came into the drawing-room at that moment and Louise noticed how tired and suddenly aged he appeared.

"Are they back already?" demanded Piers. "My father? Gerard? Is something amiss?"

Mr. Parswell was quite at home with historical antiquities, but seemed to find difficulty in putting ill-tidings into words. He stumbled and prevaricated until Piers pushed past him with an exclamation and hurried off to discover the situation at first hand.

"This is a bad business," stated Milly's father heavily and he smoothed his daughter's sleep-rumpled fair hair with trembling fingers before proceeding.

"André Durand? Where is he?" said Louise, in harsh tones, scarcely recognisable as her own. "What has he done?"

The vicar blinked at her in astonished reproof.

"Monsier Durand helped Gerard Challis to carry Sir Reginald home," he rebuked. "I hear that we have that young Frenchman to thank for his speedy attention tonight."

"Sir Reginald is hurt? I — I am sorry," whispered Louise. "Please tell us, sir! What happened? Is he — is he — ?"

"He is still alive," reassured Mr. Parswell and Milly and Louise gasped with shared relief. "There were smugglers down upon the beach. Apparently they resisted arrest and many shots were fired wildly. Sir Reginald has been badly injured and one smuggler — Beckwith, I believe they named him — is dead."

"*Raymond Beckwith*?" stammered Louise in stupefaction, an image of his plump kindly wife Annis before her eyes. How would Annis fare without her Raymond? "But he keeps the village inn, Mr. Parswell," she pursued. "Surely he was not involved — "

She fell silent, realising that she should show concern for the injured master of Challis Hall, rather than for a dead innkeeper.

"Mr. Wentworth is with his master now," said the vicar, when she faltered on to enquire of the extent of Sir Reginald's injury. "Apparently he has some medical knowledge, acquired whilst a soldier in his youth."

Louise's imagination balked at the picture of the stately butler Wentworth, with sleeves rolled up and hands stained with blood. No comment was needed, for Milly swayed upon her feet and fainted upon the drawing-room carpet, her cheeks white as death. Caring for the vicar's daughter and offering her help to the Challis family in their time of need, quickly restored Louise to Mr. Parswell's good opinion.

Yet beneath her outward show of calm control, she was bewildered and fearful. How had Raymond Beckwith, of all unlikely men, come to be shot dead as a smuggler? Why should the Frenchman, Durand, be the one to receive praise for staunching Sir Reginald's wounds and possibly saving his life by his swift attention? These two problems found her wildly incredulous. The inn-keeper had *never* been a smuggler, she told herself, remembering how Beckwith had always refused to buy contraband spirits for sale in his inn. Her confidence wavered as she acknowledged that she had only the oftrepeated words of Annis and her dead husband to assure her that they truly *had* disapproved of smuggling.

Of necessity, during his father's indisposition, Gerard Challis took charge of proceedings and Louise found herself hating the elder twin when he, filled with gratitude, installed André Durand at the Hall as a seemingly permanent guest. Gerard was loud in the Frenchman's praise and Louise was shocked to note that even her sensible Piers seemed to find no fault with the man's removal to the Hall. That *Piers*, who had kissed her and called her his love, should sway towards the enemy, was bitter news indeed and, despite her own inclination, she tried to avoid his company. She hid her unhappiness and uncertainly by throwing her full energy into plans for the future of the widowed Mrs. Beckwith.

Within a week of seeing her husband buried as an outcast on the furthest edge of the churchyard, Annis Beckwith left Challiscombe with scarcely a farewell to those who had so misjudged her beloved Raymond. The kindly woman, her plump face ravaged by grief presented Louise with an ale-mug from the inn, which had often been used by the girl's old grandfather. They wept together and for a full ten minutes Louise stared after the departed carriage, old Caleb's cracked mug held tightly in her shaking hands. Annis had been a good friend, if not a close one, to the orphaned girl, and now she was gone.

"You weep for the wife of a murderer, *m'selle*?" asked a sarcastic voice at her elbow. "The English are mad, *complètement fou*! Ah, but *are* you English, petite Héloïse-Marie?"

Louise turned to look at the handsome, sneering face of André Durand, as he stood beside her in the lane and her tears and doubts returned with a rush of feeling, so that she found difficulty in refraining from hurling the ale-mug at him. Yet there was more than a mere desire to torment and tease at her genuine grief for the bereft Annis Beckwith. He still wondered if she could be his lost Héloise-Marie! Her heart thumped unsteadily, but she managed to shake her head and speak composedly.

"My name is Louise Vaughan, sir," she said calmly enough. "You speak in riddles and I do not understand you. Naturally I grieve for poor Mrs. Beckwith. She and her husband were very happy together and his — his *death* was a considerable shock to all of us who knew him."

Durand allowed the girl to pass him and enter the vicarage grounds, but his face wore an unpleasant, calculating expression, as he turned on his heel and made his way back to Challis Hall. He could not have planned matters better! Now he was an accepted guest of the Challis family and they stood in his debt for his prompt action in succouring Sir Reginald. It was so amusing! His lip curled and he laughed shortly. That incident with the smugglers of Challiscombe Bay had been well-used! It had served to bring him into closer contact with what appeared to be his one chance to investigate the Vaughan girl and her possible past. It was evident that the girl both feared and disliked him and it was all too likely that her reasons were rooted in her knowledge of her true identity.

Durand gave another soft laugh. It had been so easy! He had thrown away his pistol that night — after its judicious use — and knew that, even if found, it could never be definitely traced back to him. Only he and that stupid innkeeper, Beckwith, had witnessed the shooting of Sir Reginald. The joke of it was that Beckwith had not even been amongst the smugglers and had only left his inn to investigate the cause of the commotion on the beach. Durand nodded with satisfaction. Naturally Beckwith had had to die! It had been suitable that the so-stupid innkeeper, with his greedy demands for payment of bills, should die blamed for Sir Reginald's injury! How easy, thought Durand, for a man of my astute brain, to pretend to aid the master of Challis Hall! Of course, the foolish Monsieur Gerard had been made to see him staunching his father's blood! How else could Sir Reginald's heir show gratitude — save by inviting the Frenchman into his home?

Everything is in my favour now, gloated André Durand. Monsieur Gerard is sensible of the debt he owes me and will not hesitate to give any aid I might require. If the Vaughan girl is really she whom I seek, then the end of my quest is in view! Nodding with self-satisfaction, the Frenchman entered Challis Hall — his present place of abode.

"You are drinking heavily, twin," observed Piers Challis, one afternoon in early December. "We never seem to talk together these days. I know you only drink when you are worried, so why not confide in me?"

Gerard emptied his brandy-glass and seemed vaguely surprised to find himself underestimating the nearness of a table. The glass rolled unharmed upon the carpet of Challis Hall library and Piers bent to pick it up, suppressing a sigh of irritation.

"Pour me another drink, Piers," asked Gerard with a scowl. "It's not your concern if I wish to be drunk as a lord! Drinking makes me forget — "

"Tell me what is wrong, Gerry," said Piers evenly and he moved the brandy-bottle from his twin's reach. "Have you been gambling again — and losing?"

"Can't gamble an' *win*!" protested Gerard pettishly. "I'm damn' sick of the whole si — situation, Piers! Father's as good as dead and that d — damn' Frenchie's using this place for his own ends. Can't do anything to stop him an' well he knows it!"

Piers regarded his brother with thoughtful distaste and rang for coffee. When the manservant had been and gone, Gerard consented to drink a cup of coffee, only to shudder violently.

"No — don't fuss like a mother-hen, twin!" he said to Piers, with a poor attempt at a smile. "Yes — you're right! You are *always* right, my dear *good* brother! I ought to hate you for it, but I can't find the strength even for that! I've gambled away my allowance for several months ahead and was fool enough to let Durand play my banker. He's like one of those damn' creeping plants that live off others and finally succeed in suffocating 'em. I'll take more coffee," he added more steadily. "I'm beginning to feel almost human again. My sensible little brother always knows what's good for me!"

"You are an idiot, Gerry!" grated Piers. "It's lucky for you that Father is still capable of dealing with money-matters from his sick-bed. If he'd been worse and you'd been named to execute his business, no doubt you'd have signed away the whole estate by now."

"I wish *you* were the elder son!" retorted the goaded Gerard. "You'd see fit to guard your inheritance better, clever old Piers!"

Piers gave him a thoughtful look and ignored the jibe.

"I agree that Durand has found himself a cosy niche in our home, Gerry," he said, "but one word to Father would soon rid us of him. Surely you don't feel burdened with him for ever?"

"Father stands too deep in the Frenchman's debt to send him off," disagreed Gerard. "*You* were not there on the beach that night, Piers. You did not see the way in which Durand ran to help Father. We'll wake up one morning, brother mine, to find our inheritance stolen from beneath our noses," he prophesied grimly. "You see if we don't!"

"The estate is entailed to you as elder son," pointed out Piers practically, "and Father is not so sick or foolish that he would sign away his fortune to André Durand! All the same, Gerry, I agree that we should speed the fellow on his way. By how much do you stand in his debt? Come, twin — the *full* amount!"

Gerard attempted prevarication, then sulkily admitted the enormity of the Frenchman's loan.

"Unless we are to tell Father of your folly, then we must find other means of raising the sum," pondered Piers. "Perhaps it would be best to tell Father, after all, for I am sure he is well enough to stand the shock."

"No!" retorted Gerard. "I'll not run to him like an errant schoolboy. We can settle this privately, I'm sure."

"Very well," agreed Piers. "How

much can you raise toward the debt, twin?"

Gerard gave an expressive shrug and a shame-faced grin.

"My allowances are all pledged to that bloodsucking Frenchie," he said, then added hopefully: "How do your finances stand, twin? You know I'll pay you back — eventually. I'd rather have *you* for banker any day!"

"And I am but the poor younger son!" said Piers with gentle sarcasm.

Gerard hunched a shoulder, trying to hide his alarm.

"Surely you are not overspent also, Piers?" he muttered.

"I could raise the necessary cash — and more," admitted Piers, "if I sell Jasper! I'm never free of offers and enquiries from would-be buyers."

Gerard Challis rose to his feet, the effects of his heavy drinking vanishing and his cheeks grew red with shame and anger. He shook his head violently.

"If you sell your beloved horse to

settle my debts, then I swear I'll end matters with a bullet in my brain!" he choked as he flung himself from the room.

Piers followed in his brother's wake and when the twins had gone, the full-length curtains which concealed an oaken window-seat, were twitched aside. A trembling, white-faced Millicent Parswell stumbled out from her hiding-place.

"I did not *mean* to eavesdrop, Louise-love!" gasped poor Milly, breathless from her headlong flight from Challis Hall to the vicarage. "Sir Reginald promised Papa the loan of a book, you see, and I was skimming through it to check I had the right one. I — I was at the window to catch the light on the pages and I did not mean to hide and listen. When I realised that Gerard and Piers were quarrelling, I tried to stop my ears and read the book — and excessively dull it was, too — all about some dead and gone town that vanished in an earthquake and should have been forgotten an age ago! Oh, Louise, what are we to *do*? Piers will sell his lovely Jasper and then Gerard — my Gerard, will shoot himself! Go to them, Louise, and bid them be sensible! Piers, at least, will listen to you!"

The younger girl subsided into a sobbing heap and Louise refused to think until she had secured a small glass of brandy to restore her friend. Milly drank it obediently, then spluttered and wept anew.

"*Brandy!*" she sobbed. "It is Gerard's downfall and now *I* am drinking it, too!"

Louise was dry-eyed and sleepless that night, deciding then rejecting the move that she alone should make. When at last pale fingers of dawn lightened the sky, she was weary with mental fatigue. Only then did she allow her tiredness to relax in sleep. But sleep brought back that same recurring nightmare and now the dream held frightening additions. André Durand was recognisably there, a miniature guillotine held in his bloodstained hands and she awoke with the certainty that she, alone, was his sought-for prey.

★　★　★

"Have you seen Louise, Papa?" asked Millicent Parswell, some days later. "I have looked everywhere and she is nowhere to be found."

A closer search revealed the dismaying fact that Louise had left the vicarage with knowing intent, for some of her clothing was gone from her room. It was not discovered until later, that. On overhearing the servant-girl, Agnes, mention the romantic suspicion that Louise might have eloped with the Frenchman, Milly smartly boxed the maid's ears, shrieked for her father, then collapsed in hysterics.

The only clue to Louise's disappearance was a note discovered in the Challis stable by Sam Trant, the head stableman. It contained a plea to Sir

Reginald for forgiveness that she had taken, without permission, a horse and a saddle. There being no personal communication for him, Piers Challis took possession of Louise's letter and the sight of tearstains on her agitatedly scrawled writing committed him to the desperate anguish of utter despair. Something Louise had once told him, echoed dully in his mind.

'Durand would go away if I said my name was really Héloise-Marie.'

Piers was convinced that these words held the explanation for Louise leaving with the Frenchman. He could not doubt that she and Durand were together and this conviction tore at his heart and mind, inflicting unbearable pain.

Now that it seemed too late, Piers Challis found himself unable to deny his love for Louise. If she came to harm at the hands of André Durand, then he knew he would not rest until the Frenchman's mangled remains lay at his feet.

"I love her!" groaned Piers to himself. "Why have I never acknowledged the true depth of my feeling for my lovely Louise? Without her, my existence will be empty indeed."

10

ALTHOUGH Sir Reginald was now up from his bed and progressing towards good health, the shadow of Louise Vaughan's disappearance lay heavily upon Challis Hall and Christmas 1802 was an unseasonably gloomy affair. Even the servants took little joy from the sight of the Yule-log blazing traditionally in the hearth. Louise had made many friends during her stay in Challiscombe and her going appeared to have increased the number of her champions. How dared anyone suggest that *their* little Miss Vaughan would leave willingly with a Frenchie? Although still outwardly at peace with France, the English countryside rippled uneasily under the threat of a new war — a possible invasion. The youngest stable-lad at Challis Hall was heard to mutter his belief that Bonaparte himself had swooped to gather up the missing girl. His elders scorned this fanciful explanation, but were obliged to admit that Louise Vaughan might never be seen again.

Millicent Parswell had set childhood resolutely behind. Her new mission in life was to try to blunt the distress of the Challis family. Piers either did not notice or chose to ignore her well-intentioned efforts, but gradually Gerard came to rely upon her new-found strength. The dawn of the new year of 1803 saw the elder twin relinquish all interest in the brandy-bottle. He began to realise that there was more to little Milly, than the insipidly pretty child he had once known with carelessly, casual affection. Milly proved herself capable of keeping house for her father and was stricter by far with the maids, than ever Louise had been. The bedroom of her absent friend was kept aired and polished in readiness for use. No one could talk Milly from the conviction that Louise would return unharmed one day.

Piers Challis spent much of his time behind closed doors with his father. The invalid was steadily regaining health and strength and frequently expressed the wish that Piers and not Gerard could be his heir. Although no one had spoken of Gerard's weakness, Sir Reginald chose to restrict his main affection, these days, to Piers, who had always been much closer to his heart.

"Sometimes I wonder if your nurse changed her infant charges from one crib to the other," said the elderly man wryly whimsical. "You were so alike as babes, she would have found the task a simple one!"

"Don't think badly of Gerry, Father," protested Piers. "He is your heir, by right of birth, and you must not forget it! Begin to rely upon his judgment and you will see how *worthy* he has become of late!" When Sir Reginald shook his greying head — he had given up his old-fashioned wig and was allowing his own hair to grow in its place — Piers nodded firmly. "Yes," went on the younger twin, "you must not place too much confidence in *me*, Father!" He smiled without amusement and added: "I imagine Gerry will wed Milly Parswell and settle down to become a model husband and provider. *I* am the more likely to cause you distress in the future. My brother has always teased me for my staid and sensible approach to life, but that was before Louise disappeared. I am afraid that my plans include nothing *sensible*, Father, but to me they are of unparalleled importance!"

"Then you still intend to go to France, my boy?" asked Sir Reginald quietly. "Can you not forget her and marry Cousin Marianne? You know that my brother plans to make you heir to his estate in Yorkshire. Marriage with your cousin would make Thomas a happy man."

"How can I forget Louise?" asked

Piers sadly. "And as for Marianne, Father — she will marry her impoverished curate, as has always been her intention. Poor Uncle Thomas will be but clay in the hands of his one remaining chick! Young Marianne has a will of her own!"

"Being strong-willed to the point of obstinacy must be a family characteristic," said his father with a shake of his head, "for there seems to be no way I can deflect *your* purpose when your mind is made up, my boy!"

"You know that I must go to Pont-Rachelle!" declared Piers. "If Durand left England with Louise then that would be his likeliest destination. If I do not find her there, then nothing — save time — will have been lost and time means little to me, Father, for I shall find her eventually, if I have to spend the rest of my life in searching!"

"Have you considered that she might not be willing to return to Challiscombe — even if she is at this Pont-Rachelle place?" asked the elderly man gently. "I can see only heartbreak ahead of you, my son, and I seem powerless to help you!"

Piers shrugged.

"If I find Louise, I shall bring her home to her rightful place," he declared. "She would never have left, if I had had the sense to speak before. She thought I dismissed her fear and distrust of Durand as mere fancies and she left because she could not rely upon my aid." Piers set his teeth into his lip, then went on bitterly: "She must have thought I did not love her enough to heed her anxiety!"

Sir Reginald Challis shook his head yet again.

"Do you see any basis for the rumour of a new war with France?" he asked next. "You must take care, my boy, for I cannot do without you. If war should break out, once you are on foreign soil then — "

"Gerard will be with you, Father," said Piers quietly, "and it will take more than Bonaparte and his forces to keep *me* from returning home!"

With this, his father had to be content, but he was filled with apprehension as he acknowledged that, after all, Piers was proving to be the more headstrong and foolhardy of his twin offspring.

★   ★   ★

The market-town was held in the grip of winter's frost, but hopeful vendors still plied their trade in the cobbled square. They blew upon their freezing hands and stamped cold feet to keep up a pretence of being warm enough to display their wares a little longer, although trade was poor today. The town had grown with the years from a small village to its present size and still possessed a duckpond. On this winter's day, no duck was foolish enough to show itself, but red-cheeked, muffled children used the frozen expanse to show off their prowess at ice-sliding. Despite the freezing cold weather, passers-by paused to smile at the healthy spectacle of the young at play.

The market-square was hemmed-in on three of its sides by small but busy shops, where anything from a crusty bread-roll to a gentleman's sword of tempered steel, might be purchased, and the outdoor traders cast many an envious look into the cheery interiors. Selling out in the open air was not a happy occupation on days like today!

Eventually the children were called in from the ice by irate parents and the less hardy of the market-traders began to pack away unsold goods. Two strangers hurried through the square, seeming intent on seeking out the warmth of a friendly hearth, but the traders were too chilled to cast more than an indifferent eye in their direction. The gentleman was fashionably-dressed and wore a heavy cloak slung casually across his shoulders to keep out the chill air. The girl, who hastened at least two strides before him, was less suitably attired in a grey gown and a thin pelisse. Her bonnetted head was down-bent, but it could be seen that the frost had nipped her nose and that her undeniably beautiful blue eyes were reddened by either cold or tears. Only one old man, hurrying to buy mulled ale to 'warm his innards' as he put it, noticed the ill-matched pair and he paused to wonder at so pretty a lass looking so unhappy.

Louise Vaughan should have been pleased that owning to the name of 'Héloise-Marie' had successfully drawn the Frenchman away from Challis-combe. Yet she was so cold and miserable that she found difficulty in concentrating on anything but her own physical distress. André Durand spoke excitedly of conveying her to France so that she could, in some magical way, uncover a hoard of treasure to satisfy his fanatical hope of a legacy from the past. Although he had not treated her with undue harshness up to now, she had no illusions of what he planned for her, once she had fulfilled her purpose. Dully, she acknowledged that he would murder her in thwarted anger when he learned that she had lied. She pondered on this with unemotional interest, knowing she could not put off the ordeal of confessing her lie, for very much longer.

Once away from Challiscombe, she had hoped to rid the Challis family and herself also, of the menace which was Durand. She had seriously considered killing the man and only his superior strength made this move impossible. Had she possessed the means to end the Frenchman's life, she would have done so without either a moral qualm or fear of retribution. He was an evil man, she thought, and a danger to those she had learned to love. But she could do nothing against his superior power, save lead him away from Challiscombe and onward towards his hoped-for goal. He was fanatically assured of the existence of untold wealth at his journey's end! At least, thought the girl, at *least* she seemed safe from any amorous attention from Durand. *That* would have been impossible to support, when her heart was filled with hopeless love for the younger Challis twin. This Héloise-Marie, who invoked some faint disturbing recognition in her own memory, appeared to be a close relative of Durand — too close for the man to dream of indulging in any form of dalliance. Louise shivered from more than exterior cold as they crossed the market-square. André Durand might call her his *petite soeur* but his chilly, near-mad expression warned that she could expect no brotherly mercy when the time came for her to admit herself powerless to aid his quest.

They left the square and Durand indicated that they should go along the town's main street. Hopelessly she plodded on in front of him, uncomforted by the promise of food and a hot reviving drink. The heavy rumble of an approaching vehicle and the clatter of hoofbeats behind them on the cobbles, underlined the oft-considered fact that she could so easily end her own life by hurling herself in the horses' path. But that, she acknowledged dully, would not rid the Challis family of the menace of André Durand. He would only return to Challiscombe, convinced that Milly Parswell and not Louise was his Héloise-Marie.

Louise cast a quick backward glance up the street, saw the huge beasts straining at the unwieldy, outmoded coach, gave an exclamation and began to run across the cobbles. Suddenly she was unable to support the pretence, with which she deceived Durand, for an instant longer. Regardless of the consequences, she would run away from the Frenchman and conceal herself where she might not be found. She would have several precious seconds to hide whilst the coach masked her from the eyes of her hated companion! Staying with Durand until he made up his mind to kill her, had lost any dubious attraction it might once have possessed. She did not wish to die!

The horses were travelling at speed and were so dangerously close, that she felt their damp breath as she fled past them. Desperately she ran beneath the arched entrance of a narrow cobbled alleyway on the other side of the road, dimly aware of Durand's shout of frustration. The Frenchman's enraged outcry was lost in a series of deafening sounds, made by splintered wood-work, reined-in horses and protesting, clamouring voices. Her feet slowed and she leaned against the wall of the alleyway, her breath coming in painful gasps. Unwillingly and against all natural instinct to flee from the scene before it was too late, she retraced her steps, only to gaze with dilated, unbelieving eyes at the horrifying sight of André Durand, the all-powerful enemy, lying trapped beneath a heavy wheel of the stationary coach. She forced herself to take a step nearer, nausea rendering her incapable of speech.

The Frenchman would frighten her no longer. The menace was irretrievably gone. Durand lay on his back, one arm twisted beneath him, the blood from his multiple wounds staining the cobbles. His face was unmarked and his eyes, no longer threatening, were open to the frosty air. He had pursued his fleeing prey, only to meet death beneath the coachwheels. Louise stared down in fascinated horror at the dead face. For an instant she saw, not André Durand, but another similar face — the face she knew from the golden locket — the face she had seen reflected mysteriously in her own mirror. This face, the same and yet subtly different, was also that of a dead man, but for him she had never felt fear, only diffident affection and the desire to please . . .

The scene blurred before her staring eyes as knowledge, hitherto concealed, rushed in and overwhelmed her. Demands that the coach be moved, a plea to have those dead eyes covered, protests from the coach-driver, all jostled for importance. But Louise Vaughan heard none of them. She sank down on to the bloodstained cobbles, dropped her head into her hands and began to sob. A sympathetic by-stander lifted the girl to her feet and propelled her away from the scene of the accident.

"Chasing the poor girl, he was!" declared an old woman rustily. "Served him right! You can see from his fine clothes as he was a gentleman and she but an ordinary maid. Frightened you, did he, my pretty? Well, he'll frighten no one again!"

"Was he a friend, missy?" asked another concerned voice. "Who was he?"

Louise lifted her head and cast a haunted look about her at the ring of surrounding faces. Mercifully, she could no longer see André Durand's body.

"A — a *friend*?" she echoed unsteadily. "No, he was not a friend of mine! I — I do not believe I knew him at all!"

She began to shake with hysterical laughter, not unmixed by tears and the crowd decided charitably that the poor girl was suffering from shock. An accident like that was enough to shock anyone, was it not?

* * *

Piers Challis dismounted, then stood quietly beside black Jasper, the reins held loosely in one hand. This clifftop was the exact spot from where he had watched Caleb Vaughan ten long years ago. The scene was unchanged except by the hour and season. The boy Piers had come to watch the sun rise over Challiscombe Bay and it had been springtime. He had seen Caleb Vaughan discover a wrecked boat on the chain of rocks and the sight of a child clasped in the old man's arms, had been the start of the boy's involvement with a mystery.

The man Piers looked down today to see the beach concealed by choppy, white-maned waves. Occasionally a long, unbroken wall of grey water swelled landwards, only to disintegrate into a flying curtain of spray, as it met the jagged threat of those very rocks where Vaughan had found the boat. The ten-year-old mystery of the boat, the dead man and the child still remained unsolved.

Piers had been unable to persuade anyone to take him across to France until winter's reign was safely past. Even the local smugglers — several of whom he had tentatively approached — had refused to risk life and limb until at least the month of February was out. Piers scuffed his booted feet on tufted grass, made harsh and brittle by winter's frost and unwillingly he accepted the necessity of a delay, before he could seek out the place called Pont-Rachelle. He knew little enough about his proposed destination but was not to be deterred from his purpose. Sir Reginald had reluctantly supplied the information that Comte Henri had once possessed a *chateau* in Normandy and this was Piers' one frail clue to the whereabouts of Pont-Rachelle. The revolution would have wrought dire change and Piers disliked the thought of what he might find. Only the hope that his lovely Louise would be at the end of the journey made Piers Challis refuse to contemplate the threat of a new war. If Louise Vaughan were not to be found in France and if Bonaparte's manoeuvres blocked the return to England, *then* would be the time for concern, mused Sir Reginald's younger son. Yet if he did not find and bring home Louise, his own possible fate in enemy territory would be of little account, thought Piers grimly.

Jasper began to fidget restlessly and the horse's snorting breath caused clouds of steam in the frosty air. In the act of remounting, Piers became suddenly still, his intent gaze directed down towards old Vaughan's deserted cottage. It had fallen into disrepair and held an air of forgotten neglect, yet today the door stood ajar! Piers stared in disbelief and Jasper strained away in eager impatience for the warmth of his stable.

With an angry exclamation, Piers secured his mount by tangling the reins in a weathered gorse bush. Yes, the cottage door was open! That some worthless vagabond should enter what had once been the home of Louise Vaughan, was almost an act of sacrilege and certainly not to be countenanced. Piers set off irefully down the sloping path, whilst Jasper chewed disconsolately at the unrewarding bush. The black horse had had enough of his master's tardiness and wanted only to return home.

Piers approached the open door of the cottage, still angry, but prepared against possible attack from the unlawful occupant. He listened intently, then kicked the door wide. A stifled scream of undoubtedly feminine origin greeted his ears and he gazed with stupefied amazement into the shadowed blue eyes of the girl he had thought to be in France.

"*Louise!*" he managed, then advanced with outstretched arms. "Oh my *love!*"

Louise backed from him warily and his shocked eyes took in the ragged state of her clothing and the tangled locks of her normally shining hair.

"No!" she gasped. "Do not touch me! Keep away or I will — I will — "

She cast a wild look around her as if seeking for a weapon and Piers became as still as if carved from stone.

"Louise," he said again. "Louise — do you not know me, love?"

She blinked dazedly, then rubbed at her eyes and took an unsteady step towards him.

"P — Piers?" she whispered. "Oh, *Piers!*"

Moving suddenly, she set old Caleb Vaughan's chair between herself and the man in the doorway. Desperately she shook her head.

"Listen to me, Piers," she said in a low shaken voice. "First I must tell you what has happened."

Piers Challis clenched his hands against his sides and remained still with difficulty.

"Where is that damned Frenchman, Louise?" he said curtly. "What has he done to put that look into your eyes, love? What has he done, to make you turn even from *me*? I swear I will kill him if — "

The girl seemed suddenly seized by mirth.

"Kill him?" she said hysterically. "Oh, but it is too late for that! It is far too l — late, Piers! André Durand is dead. He died in December soon after we left Challiscombe. He c — can't hurt any of us again!"

"Durand is dead?" queried Piers gently.

Louise shuddered and did not resist when Piers took her firmly by the shoulders.

"Horribly dead!" she murmured. "You see, I led him away from here and I p — planned to kill him. I said I was called Héloise-Marie and he was taking me to France." She stared unseeingly across the dimness of the cottage and went on without expression: "I wanted him dead, but he was too strong for me! I could do nothing and I tried to run away. He ran after me and was c — crushed under a coach!" She looked up at Piers, her eyes wide and shocked. "I caused his death after all and I am glad — do you hear, Piers? I am glad, glad, *glad* that it was my fault he died!"

Suddenly she struggled to be free and Piers Challis tightened his grip upon her shoulders.

"My poor little love!" he murmured. "Oh, Louise — why did you go away? Could you not have turned to me?"

"You did not believe how evil he was," said the girl with a heavy sigh. "Let me go, Piers! I will dirty your coat! I am not a fit person for you to know — "

"Be still, love," warned Piers, as he drew her more gently towards him. "You will only be hurt if you try to escape me now! How could you be so heartless to leave me without word, my Lou? You cannot imagine the torment I have suffered."

"But you were all so good to me," she murmured against his coat. "How could I repay your kindness by allowing that — that *devil* to threaten you? It is well that he is dead, Piers! I knew he would kill me eventually and at first I did not care, but then — "

"We have talked enough of death!" said Piers chidingly. "Life is too sweet for you to talk so, love. If Durand is dead, then it was an accident and you must not blame yourself. We must forget the past and plan now for the future — *our* future, Louise!"

"Death took him by surprise," she went on as if Piers had not spoken. "I was running away and he thought I could lead him to a fortune. He was strong, but not strong enough to live beneath the weight of that coach — "

"Hush!" ordered Piers, hugging her shivering form closely to him. "If you must continue to explain, then do so later. I am taking you home now, love! Come, Jasper is waiting outside and he soon grows impatient when he is left alone."

"Home?" she murmured vaguely. "Yes, I suppose that would be sensible. You see, I am so tired — so *very* tired — "

He lifted her unresisting form into his arms and went up the cliff path to the waiting black horse. It was unfortunate, thought Piers grimly, that André Durand should have died before the full extent of his harm to Louise had been revealed. I hope, said the kindly courteous Piers Challis to himself with unprecedented viciousness, I hope he died in agony.

Back in the warm cleanliness of her own room at the vicarage, Louise came gradually out of her state of shock and wept weakly to realise how she had gloried in the ghastly death of a fellow human-being. She told Piers and Milly of how she had been given shelter after the Frenchman's death. A kindly woman had taken her into her home, but Louise had slowly become aware that she was degenerating into the woman's unpaid drudge. This realisation had resulted in her trudging penniless back to the cliffside cottage left to her by old Caleb. She had no clear idea of the many miles she had been obliged to walk in the freezing winter weather, but spoke thankfully of the kindly farmer who had conveyed her for the last part of her journey upon his open cart.

Piers would have had her forget the past, but she spoke at length upon the subject of André Durand and his belief in a legacy of riches. He had suspected that she was his half-sister, Héloise-Marie du Pont-Rachelle. To lead him away from Challiscombe, she had finally agreed that she was indeed the Frenchman's lost relative. No, she assured Piers, she had not met physical harm at Durand's hands.

Piers sat at her bedside in frowning disbelief and Milly Parswell hovered in the background to play chaperone, as the tale was further unfolded.

"I know that I am neither Héloise-Marie, nor any other connection of your father's lost Barbara, Piers," went on Louise. "You see, I can remember it all now! I am merely one of Comte Henri's many illegitimate offspring. I am nothing!" Piers frowned at this and Milly shook her head in distress. "But Héloise-Marie was the comte's legitimate daughter — the child of Comtesse Barbara. I called her Héli and I knew her well. Durand did not seem to know what had happened to poor little Héli — and nor did I until my memory of those days returned to me!"

"Will you not rest now, love?" asked gentle Milly persuasively. "You are upsetting yourself unnecessarily, Louise! It is all over now and you are home and safe!"

Louise sat up in bed, her cheeks unnaturally flushed.

"No!" she choked. "I cannot be silent! I must speak of all that has happened. I will never rest easy until —"

"Go on with your story, Louise," encouraged Piers, with a warning shake of the head to the troubled Milly. "Come — we are both listening."

Louise gave him a trembling smile.

"I — I knew that you would understand, Piers," she said. Her smile faded and she drew in a shuddering breath. "Little Héli was killed when the mob burst in to carry the comtesse — to — to the guillotine. I was there, but no one saw me. I was hiding in a cupboard and peering through a crack in the wood! I saw poor Héli, lying face-down with blood on her hair. She was dead and — and they took away Comtesse Barbara. She was so brave and so proud and she walked off in their midst with her head held high —" Louise fell silent and dropped her head into her hands, as if to shut out the crowding images of past horror. For a moment all was quiet and then she looked up and continued more collectedly: "My true name is Lucette Latour. My mother was sewing-maid to the comtesse and the comte married her off to a man called Latour, when he knew she was to have his child. Comte Henri was well-used to marrying off his discarded women! André Durand's background was similar to that of mine but there was a significant difference between us.

"My step-father, Michel Latour, was detailed at the height of the Terror to take little Héli to safety in England with Comtesse Barbara's people. But Héli died, so he set off with *me* instead. Perhaps he hoped to pretend to the English relatives that I was their grand-child. I will never know what he planned. I remember shots being fired as I helped him to launch the boat. It was very dark and I was terrified, but we escaped and put out to sea. I — I was unharmed but he must have been injured by gunshot, because he died later. I remember little more, but I know now that the boat was washed up in Challiscombe Bay — where dear Granfer Caleb found me."

Louise was silent at last and Milly Parswell took one of her friend's limp hands as it lay on the bed coverlet. Piers Challis was very much aware that his poor Louise would only regain peace of mind if she were allowed to relive the horror of all that was past. Despite his inclination to call a halt to her revelations, he quietly bade her continue. Milly opened her mouth to protest, then gave a reluctant nod. Milly had grown up in her friend's absence. It would be mere childish weakness to ask Louise to forget the past, she acknowledged wisely.

"What was this 'significant difference' between your position and that of André Durand, love?" queried Piers, as Louise stared blankly ahead.

"Oh!" she whispered. "Oh, yes! I must go on and tell you about André. Well, although I was Comte Henri's acknowledged daughter, I had never been brought up in expectation of anything beyond my place as companion to my half-sister Héli. I knew her from birth," said Louise simply, a faraway look in her blue eyes, "for I was two years her senior. But André's case was different. He was a lively, handsome boy and Comte Henri promised to make full provision for him when he grew to manhood. You see, after many years of marriage, little Héli was the only child and Comte Henri had no legitimate male heir. André was the acknowledged favourite and he was reared in the nursery of the chateau, because his mother died at his birth."

Louise paused again and looked from Milly's anxious face to the stillness that was Piers Challis.

"Durand's behaviour is becoming clear to me," agreed Piers at last, with a smile that dispelled his trance-like attitude.

"Yes," said Louise dully. "But I am

still glad that he is dead, Piers. Whatever his childhood background led him to expect, it cannot excuse his threat to ruin the happiness of your family." She continued before Piers could speak. "André Durand considered himself sole heir to Chateau Pont-Rachelle. He told me of his fanatical obsession with a legacy from the past and he intended to use my knowledge of the chosen hiding-place of the family's heirlooms, to regain his rightful position. He spoke of all of this quite openly, once I had said I was really Héli. I said I would go with him to France and help him to find the family heirlooms. I would have promised anything to get him away from Challiscombe! He was mad, you see, Piers, and he was dangerous to you and your ailing father. I had to go with him! I doubt that anyone had time to think about concealing valuables in the chateau, in that terrible time, but he was convinced that a legacy awaited him in France. Yes — he was mad! My own memories are from the viewpoint of a young child, but I know that Madame la Comtesse had lost all interest in life when her husband was taken away weeks earlier. My step-father, Michel Latour, took the gold locket from Héli's corpse in the con-fusion of that shocking day and he fastened it about my neck. I can remember protesting and screaming and being cuffed on the head by Latour. I think that he and I were pretending to join the mob in looting the chateau. I can recall the whole building being set to the torch," she stopped with a choked sob and hid her face in the pillow.

"We must not tax her strength too far, Piers," pleaded Milly. "I will give her a posset to make her sleep. Come away, for I'm sure we know more than enough of this horrific tale. Oh — it is no wonder you had nightmares, Louise-love!" she said, stroking her friend's hand.

Louise sat up resolutely in her bed.

"I'm almost to the end," she said more composedly. "André Durand was convinced that his supposed legacy must lie hidden in the ruined chateau. He told me that he — he joined the revolutionaries and abandoned all aristocratic claim until about four years ago, when he learned by chance that his half-sister, Héloise-Marie, might be alive and in England. He saw her both as a claimant to his hoped-for legacy and as a means of directing him to its location. Apparently he went to Pont-Rachelle before coming to England and found the chateau to be an uninhabited shell. I shall hate his memory forever, for his coming to England," she said passionately.

"He learned of Comtesse Barbara's link with Challiscombe?" suggested Piers. "He came here to find out if the child had been taken in by my father — the man Barbara had left behind?"

"I suppose the rest is obvious," said Louise and a solitary tear trickled down her pale cheek. "Durand came to

Challiscombe and learned that a harmless old man by the name of Caleb Vaughan had a mysteriously acquired grandchild. Granfer died saying that his attacker was like the man in the locket, Piers, as you will remember."

"Caleb must have looked inside the locket and then hidden it away with the empty box," agreed Piers. He rose to his feet and shook his head. "This ordeal has been too much for you, love," he said. "Milly will get you a posset as she promised and then you must sleep."

He bent over the bed and put his lips gently to her brow. Louise reached out to clutch at his hand and the look in her eyes told him he would never again need to doubt her feeling for him.

"André Durand beat a helpless old man to death, just to satisfy his mad obsession," she said bleakly. "He — he boasted of this to me and that was when I decided to kill him. But the coachwheels cheated me!"

Milly Parswell drew in her breath

279

sharply in a suppressed gasp but Piers did not seem shocked by his love's vehemence.

"Caleb Vaughan never hated a living soul, Louise," he reminded her quietly. "You will betray all the years of love that the old man gave to you, if you are weak enough to hate Durand. The Frenchman is dead, gone, unimportant and not worthy of any strong emotion. Let the matter rest there!"

Louise sighed and gave a slow, considering nod. She looked from Piers to the anxious Milly.

"Piers is always right, is he not, Milly?" she asked with the ghost of a smile. "Yes, fetch me that posset and I promise I will try to sleep."

The vicar's daughter hurried off to prepare the hot drink with her own hands and Louise turned back to Piers, her smile fading.

"When one thing has been accomplished, Piers, I will endeavour to forget the past," she said heavily. "But there is still something that must be done."

He moved to sit on the edge of the bed, an action which would have scandalised the absent Milly, and took Louise's hand in a reassuring clasp.

"You are determined to go back to Pont-Rachelle?" he said.

She was unsurprised that he should read her thoughts with such accuracy.

"My own mother, Jeannine Latour, may still be alive," she said levelly. "You can see why I must go back there, Piers! I care nothing for Durand's mythical legacy, but I must discover if my only relative survived the burning of Chateau Pont-Rachelle!"

★ ★ ★

Louise's swift recovery from the effects of shock and the weary journey back to Challiscombe, seemed little short of miraculous, but Piers knew that she was driving herself almost beyond endurance, so that she might be well enough to travel to France. He feared the result of her inner conflict might lead to total physical collapse, but could not dissuade her from what was, to her, the only possible course of action. He could not keep her here, except by the doubtful means of brute force and so, with a sense of inevitable doom, he began to make the necessary preparations for the journey — a journey which promised to be both exhausting and dangerous.

"But, twin!" expostulated Gerard. "This is madness! It was different when you thought Louise was in France, but she is home now and safe in England! Why jeopardise both your lives by going abroad now that war seems imminent? Remember that although Louise might be French, *you* are English and your nationality might well prove to be your undoing. Boney hates the English! Oh, this is all so unnecessary, you idiot!"

"And what has Bonaparte to do with it?" chaffed Piers. "You speak as if you expect us to meet, face to face, the little Coriscan and I!"

Gerard Challis shook his head at

what he considered quite unsuitable levity under the circumstances.

"Then," said the elder twin at length, "I suppose I must offer to come with you!" He looked at his brother with admiring respect. "I never thought you had it in you, to be so idiotically *brave*, brother mine!"

"You will stay at home with Father," said Piers mildly enough, yet with a glint of steel in his grey eyes. "He cannot support the shock of losing both of us! No — I must take Louise, for she is not to be thwarted in her aim. One of the vicarage maids, Carrie, has volunteered to go with us to play chaperone."

"*Chaperone?*" echoed Gerard with a shake of his head. "Why not have Louise wed you, here and now — for I know that's your intention in the long term! You could then exert a husband's rights and forbid her to risk her life abroad! Twin," he cleared his throat gruffly, "I've no wish to sit safely at home and wait for news of your death!"

Piers smiled at this genuine concern for his safety.

"Nor do I wish to die, Gerry," he agreed lightly. "Come — this is only an exploratory expedition, after all! I do not intend to declare war on Bonaparte personally!"

Gerard frowned, unappeased.

"For all your foolery, twin," he said, "we know that a fresh declaration of war with France must come. This so-called peace is a strange, uneasy affair."

"Then that is all the more reason for you to stay at home," reasoned Piers. "You are Father's heir and a certain responsibility rests upon your shoulders."

His tone was persuasive and devoid of any bitterness when he spoke of his brother's future inheritance. Gerard nodded unwillingly, then smiled.

"Uncle Thomas is bound to will you his Yorkshire estate, twin," he said, "so do not talk like the penniless younger son! When Cousin Marianne marries her curate, our uncle will not see them starve, but nor will he empty his coffers to support the pair of them in luxury! No — the manor and farm and all that go with them, will one day be yours. Your future will be far from poverty-stricken!"

"At this moment, it is only the *immediate* future that worries me, Gerry," confessed Piers wryly, "but Louise would set off to France alone, if I refused to take her there."

"She is the most stubborn female I have ever met," agreed Gerard with resignation. "Well, twin, there is nothing left but to wish you both a successful journey and a safe return! I hope you will not be away long, for I know that Milly will have me on my knees beside her in church, praying for you, for the whole of your absence!"

The brothers parted amicably and Piers went to make his peace with Sir Reginald, knowing that gentleman found difficulty in resigning himself to the necessity of the venture — now that Louise had returned home.

11

THE small, but intrepid, party of three set sail from harbour in Dorset and the crossing of the English Channel was accomplished with nothing more momentous than Carrie's suffering from seasickness. But *that*, declared the little maid stoutly, was nothing when compared with the wonderful chance of seeing the world beyond her native village of Challiscombe! Piers hoped the girl's loyalty and enthusiasm would not be rewarded by a fresh outbreak of war that would keep her permanently far from home. He knew that one or more of his father's menservants would have willingly gone with them to France, but judged that the larger the party the more they would resemble an invasion-force — should they be taken for foreigners. As matters stood, he hoped they might progress towards the place called Pont-Rachelle, without being challenged to state their business.

He was pleased to see Louise with colour in her cheeks, as she recovered some of her former beauty, but he accepted that she would not lose those shadows from beneath her dark-blue eyes until her inner peace was restored. He was learning, he thought with wry humour, to accept everything about this strange situation. It was fortunate that his nature had always been more placid and less volatile than that of his twin brother, Gerard! Gerard would never have had the patience to trek with two dependent females across foreign soil!

Once in France they assumed the identity of French *émigrés* returning from exile — in case of any form of questioning which might possibly arise. Carrie had been warned to keep a close hold on her tongue. Although Louise was bi-lingual and Piers could speak passable French, the little Devonshire maidservant could not understand a single word of what she privately termed 'Froggy-talk'. Carrie was a sensible girl and knew full well the dangers of her ignorance, but her care and thoughtfulness towards Louise made her a worthy member of this expedition abroad.

They saw more than one ruined dwelling of past grandeur as they journeyed onwards and Piers was fearful of the final outcome, when Louise must come face to face with the state in which the Revolution had left Chateau Pont-Rachelle. Even if Jeannine Latour had survived the assault upon the chateau and still lived in the district, the full answer to Louise's anxiety might not be received.

They jogged on in the horse-drawn cart Piers had hired some miles back and, as the taciturn driver paused to point his whip as they neared yet another village Louise gave a sudden shuddering sigh. Piers frowned in alarm at her pallor.

"We are here?" he whispered in French.

She clasped her hands until the knuckles showed white and gave a convulsive nod of her head.

"Yes, Pierre," she said, speaking in the same tongue and using the name they had chosen for him as more suited to his supposed nationality. "That church — those cottages — I have seen them all before."

"Pont-Rachelle!" grunted the driver, with a take-it-or-leave-it air. He slid down from his seat and left Piers to assist the womenfolk. "You require that I wait, *m'sieur?*" he enquired, as he pocketed his tip.

Piers raised an eyebrow at Louise, who was trembling as she looked beyond the untidily-grouped houses, obviously searching for a first glimpse of the chateau. Slowly she shook her head.

"Thank you, but no," said Piers. "We will remain here for a time."

"If you change your mind, *m'sieur*,

you will find me at the inn," said the driver, made garrulous by the money he had received. He scratched his unshaven chin raspingly and added with a shrug: "Pont-Rachelle offers nothing. It was the home of *ci-devant* aristos and met its natural fate."

Piers drew in a steadying breath and offered his arm to Louise, as he gave the wide-eyed Carrie a reassuring smile. The three of them were weary and travel-stained and their arrival appeared to have aroused no interest in the local inhabitants. Perhaps the inn, a shabby-looking building of dubious comfort, might provide them with refreshment and washing-water, he thought hopefully. But the sight of Louise's white, drawn expression, warned him that she did not intend even a momentary delay before they sought out the chateau. He patted the hand she rested so trustingly upon his arm and tried to forget the length of time which had elapsed since they had last eaten.

Pont-Rachelle held a poverty-stricken

air, which the maid Carrie secretly compared with the comfort of her home village of Challiscombe. She saw a dog scratching at the stony soil, its rib-cage visible through its mangy coat. When the girl moved a sympathetic hand in the creature's direction, it snarled and sprang at her. But for the swift intervention of Piers Challis, Carrie might have been maimed for life. Piers swung her aside, picked up a knotted stick and threatened the beast until it slunk off, shoestring tail between its legs.

"The village has changed," observed Louise, when she had comforted poor bewildered Carrie. "I remember flowers in the cottage-gardens and children playing in the streets. Everything is so neglected and — *and dead.*"

No children were to be seen and the air of desolation lasted until they reached the last cottage. In its doorway sat a broad-shouldered man, who rose and came towards them. His home was well-tended and clean, but his expression was forbidding as he faced them, huge thumbs hooked into the broad leather belt at his waist. Although no longer young, he was a powerfully-built fellow and exceeded Piers Challis' not-inconsiderable height by at least two inches. Hunger and weariness made Piers hope that the man intended no physical menace upon them.

"This road leads nowhere," he said in a surly tone. "Turn and go back the way you came or — "

"*Chateau Pont-Rachelle!*" breathed Louise. "Look, Piers! Look, Carrie! The castle still stands!"

They stared at the enormous grey monument to past workmanship and indeed, from this angle, it appeared to be unharmed and intact, apart from obvious damage to the tops of its turrets and towers. On this dull March day, the chateau seemed formidably impregnable, for all it had brought to life a dormant joy in Louise Vaughan. It was situated beyond a belt of trees and had been hidden from view until they rounded the final cottage. A stream of pewter-grey water, spanned by an ancient stone bridge, flowed past the leafless trees, adding to the uninviting scene.

Piers saw a questioning frown on the brow of the giant of a man who blocked their path and he realised that, in her excitement, Louise had forgotten to speak in French.

"Foreigners?" grated the man suspiciously. "Turn back, I say. There is nothing for you at Pont-Rachelle! The chateau was fired ten years ago. Nothing remains but a crumbling outer wall. The inside is a blackened ruin."

Piers caught the man's meaning, but found difficulty in translating the heavy, peasant dialect into the precise French he had learned (and partially forgotten) at school. To his alarm, Louise moved suddenly and put a fearless hand upon the man's sleeve, smiling up at him.

"You cannot have forgotten me, Gaspard?" she asked accusingly. "See I am Lucette Latour and I have come back to find my mother! Piers — all is well! This is only my good friend, Gaspard Villon."

Slowly and bemusedly the man eyed her up and down, then a gap-toothed grin transformed his aggressive appearance.

"Then you did not die, little Lucette?" he said as he grasped her hands in his huge ones. "You are grown to be a handsome woman!"

Piers and Carrie watched in relief as Louise and Gaspard Villon chatted on incomprehensibly. At first, Villon expressed reluctance and there was much shaking of his grizzled head and much determined nodding of Louise's dark curls.

"Very well," said Villon at length. "But no harm must come to the *Chateau des Orphélines*! I will take you, but mark all I have told you, Lucette Latour!"

"What did he tell you, Louise?" asked Piers in English, when he was at last able to claim her attention. "Is your mother to be found inside the castle?" He quickened his step to keep level with the girl, as she began to speed after Gaspard Villon down the road to the bridge. Carrie trotted on in their wake and they crossed the bridge over the turgidly-flowing grey water of the stream. Silently Carrie condemned the castle as a nasty old ruin and hoped she would not be obliged to enter it. "Louise," persevered Piers, "why did Villon call it the *Chateau des Orphélines*? It is a strange name for an uninhabited ruin, love!"

Piers fell silent, his questions unanswered, as they approached a massive wooden door in the looming wall of the chateau. They stood, dwarfed to insignificance by the vastness of what had once been a mighty stronghold.

"Oh, we're surely not going inside, Miss Louise?" asked Carrie in a subdued whisper. "Is it safe? Look at the size of those blocks of stone in the walls! I've never seen the like of it, in all my days!"

Gaspard Villon beat a rhythmic

tattoo on a panel of the great door and they heard the sound repeated from the other side, as if in echo. There was a rattle of bolts being withdrawn and several minutes went by, before the door was opened a fraction. Despite the seriousness of the situation, Piers Challis found difficulty in suppressing a smile at the dramatic secrecy. He lost all amusement when he followed the others into the chateau. The door clanged shut behind them and Gaspard Villon nodded with pardonable pride as the newcomers gasped with amazement.

He had spoken the truth when he told them that fire had destroyed all but the sheltering outer walls. The knowledge he had withheld was that a veritable village of dwellings had been built from reclaimed stone, within the original confines of the chateau. A flat, grassy area, which might once have been a courtyard, held the pleasant picture of sheep grazing with their white-fleeced lambs. Everywhere the visitors looked, they were met by the inquisitive faces of bright-eyed children. An older girl could be seen, milking a cow inside a lean-to shed. Newly-washed garments were set to dry upon a wall. Some of the primitive little houses even possessed a patch of garden, where vegetables might be grown at the correct season. From even a first glimpse, it was evident that the supposed ruin contained a thriving, self-supporting community.

Louise turned at last to Piers, her dark-blue eyes a-glow.

"All of this," she said, spreading her arms to encompass her surroundings, "was made possible by one woman! Piers, I can be proud to call myself Latour!"

"Your mother, Jeannine Latour, founded this — er — settlement?" he asked in bewilderment.

"Yes!" said Louise, as she hugged the staring Carrie with happy abandon. "*My mother* did this! You will see many children here. Gaspard says this is why the place has earned the name of 'castle of orphans'. My mother found so many orphaned children when the ashes of the fire had cooled and the Pont-Rachelle family were gone, that she swore she would put the chateau to a worthy use. But, Piers — *how* she has succeeded at this gigantic task! She must have a will of iron! I am half-afraid to meet her. Gaspard has gone to announce the news that we are here. He is self-appointed guardian to the chateau, you see, and always fobs off would-be explorers with the tale that it is just an empty shell. Piers — I feel quite dizzy with excitement!"

"You are not alone in that!" said Piers dryly.

Deep down in the midst of his amazement at the remarkable achievement of Jeannine Latour, was a growing apprehension that would not be denied. Louise's happy delight saddened him intolerably. Would she ever agree to return with him to Challiscombe, or would she plead to stay with her new-found mother in the peaceful unreality of this small world within the sheltering arms of the dead chateau? He gave himself a mental shake, determined not to spoil her pleasure in the hopeful reunion with her mother. This should be a joyful day and should not be marred by his brooding on problems which had not yet materialised!

"Gaspard and his friends in the village provide all necessary items that cannot be produced in here," said Louise. "Oh! Never in my wildest dreams did I guess at the surprise in store for us! See — there are cows to give milk and sheep to give wool and vegetable-patches for growing food! Nothing has been neglected. Everything needed for a happy existence can be seen here!"

If possible, Piers Challis felt his heart sink even lower, but he forced himself to smile, although words were at present beyond him.

"You'm right, Miss Louise," said Devonshire Carrie, infected by her mistress' enthusiasm. "Look — there are chickens over there, so that means eggs an' fowls for the table. Who'd have believed all of *this* could be in the middle of this great ruin? Why, there's means here to stand siege, even from that old Boney himself!"

Piers forebore to voice the thought that the inhabitants of the *Chateau des Orphélines* were French and that old Boney' was not the enemy in this part of the world. Yet, Carrie was right. A self-productive strong-hold such as this could stand any threat of invasion — especially if its presence were unsuspected. Up to now, Piers had seen only women and children here, except for the ancient fellow who had opened the door to the visitors. Piers hoped fervently that his party from England *was* only on a visit to this fantastic place. He wondered practically how Jeannine Latour, once a humble maid in the chateau, had come by the necessary capital to found this community. She must be a truly remarkable woman!

It was ten years since the burning of the chateau, reflected Piers. Jeannine's original *orphélines* must now be young adults. Were they still sworn to secrecy as to the chateau's true purpose? Piers frowned to himself. Even if matters had proceeded smoothly thus far, Jeannine Latour must realise that this small world of her own creation must one day stand revealed. It seemed incredible that none save Gaspard Villon and his friends should be aware of the secret life within the ancient walls of Chateau Pont-Rachelle!

Incredible or no, mused Piers, the dead uninhabited appearance of the outer walls had deceived *him*, when he had crossed the bridge that spanned the stream beyond the village. Small wonder that Pont-Rachelle village wore a neglected air, when the true throbbing pulse of the community was here, concealed inside these protective, time-weathered ramparts!

A hushed whisper of disbelief from Louise, interrupted Piers at this point in his reverie. The girl gripped at his arm and the eager, expectant glow of discovery ebbed away to leave her pale and shivering. She began to stammer incoherently.

"What is it, love?" he asked, putting an arm about her shoulders. "Come, tell me what has frightened you. What can you have seen to upset you in this small paradise?"

She did not respond to his teasing tone, but clung to him wordlessly. They had paused outside one of the simple cottages and Piers glanced inside to see a sparsely-furnished but spotlessly clean interior. He could see nothing to account for the change in Louise.

"No, not in there," managed the girl at last, her voice muted with shock and incredulity. "Piers — look at the girl over there. Yes, the one who is playing with those children. Tell me I am wrong! Tell me I am asleep and dreaming all of this, for it just cannot be true!"

Piers stared obediently across the

grass, past the frisking lambs, to where a brown-haired girl of medium height was skipping with a ring of children, their linked hands obviously beating out the rhythm of a song they were singing.

"L — Let us wander casually over there," begged Louise, her eyes dark and enormous in her pale face and her fingers pressing painfully into Piers' arm. "I must see her more closely before I can be certain — "

Piers complied with this odd request and he experienced a twinge of his former apprehension. From the tense, watchful expression on Louise's face, he found it easy to believe that *this* moment, the sight of *this* girl, was the sole answer to their quest. Yet Jeannine Latour must be considerably older than the young female who held Louise's rapt attention.

The girl seemed to be about seventeen years of age and she wore a simple, grey-stuff gown. Her face was not exactly pretty, but she had an inner glow which transformed her looks to almost unearthly beauty. Piers was surprised with his fanciful notion and decided that Jeannine Latour's miniature paradise must have addled his brain.

The game ended and some of the children scampered away. As if she knew she was being watched, the girl turned to face them, one small boy's hand still trustingly in hers. Her eyes were of a wide light blue and were completely blank of any emotion, although her lips still framed a smile. For an instant, those clear expressionless eyes were directed at the silent trio from England, then the girl bent her head to listen to the child. She nodded and skipped off with him across the grass and out of sight round a cottage.

"Y — yes!" breathed Louise faintly. "Yes, it is Héli! Piers — that girl is Héloise-Marie du Pont-Rachelle! But Héli died on the night I left the chateau. I saw her dead with my own eyes!"

"She is Marie, *l'ange aux orphélines*!" contradicted a harsh voice at Piers' elbow. "Who are you? Why do you trespass in our kingdom?"

Carrie gave a frightened scream and Piers himself was scarcely reassured by the fact that the wild-eyed apparition at his side was speaking partly in rusty unaccustomed English. He thrust the shrieking Carrie behind him and reached out to do the same to Louise. This female amazon with her draggled locks of iron-grey hair was mad as Bedlam! He frantically searched his mind for something to say that suited this unparalleled occasion, but the sight of pale March sunshine, glinting on the blade of a long knife clutched in the bony hand of this formidable harridan, robbed him of the power of speech.

It was Louise who finally broke the seemingly eternal silence and her voice trembled with an emotion that was — amazingly — not one of fear.

"*Maman*?" she said tentatively, as she looked again on the face of the woman whose image had shown itself so fleetingly in her mirror in Challiscombe vicarage. "Maman — can it really be you, after all these years?"

The woman narrowed her eyes to slits.

"Then you *are* Lucette, as that idiot Villon told me?" she said shortly and Piers was relieved to see the hand that held the knife drop to her side. "Why have you come here?" went on the brusque, uncompromising tone. "If you expect to tell my secret to the world — " she raised the knife to her own throat, but fortunately this horrid gesture was merely symbolic — or so Piers hoped.

"But, Maman — I am your daughter, Lucette," faltered Louise. "Have you no word of welcome? I have travelled many miles to be with you again."

"*Maman,* she calls me," mocked Jeannine Latour.

"Pah! I am not mother to you! Come — we will talk in my house!"

Poor little Carrie was almost swooning with terror and Piers could not decide whether to drag the girl with him as he followed the shocked and obedient Louise, or to leave her out on the grass with the familiar saneness of the laughing children. Carrie settled the matter herself by grabbing hold of Piers' hand in a way which proclaimed not master and maid, but fellow-sufferers in a foreign prison. This whimsy did nothing to reassure Piers, as they pursued the vanishing figures of Louise and Jeannine Latour, but he let the girl's hand rest in his.

The house was no different in size from that of its neighbours but, once inside its door, the woman Louise unbelievably addressed as "mother" shed some of her wildness. Indeed she seemed almost civilised when she quietly bade them sit on wooden stools beside the hearth, where a low fire was burning.

"When the fools outside see smoke from our fires, they believe they see spectres of that smoke of long ago — smoke from the burning of the chateau. It is a superstition for which we can thank Gaspard Villon. He is a good friend, that one! You will take coffee?"

she went on, for all the world as if this were a normal courtesy-call upon a normal household. "Perhaps you would prefer to have wine?"

Meekly Piers asked for wine, but he judged that it would take at least half a bottle of brandy to restore his scattered wits. Carrie choked upon the wine, for she was unused to such luxury, but Louise refused all sustenance and eyed Jeannine Latour levelly.

"Maman," she protested with a ghost of a smile, "maman, you acted so convincingly that I — that we were frightened."

"H'mm," said the woman. "So you are no fool, *ma fille*?" She nodded suddenly towards Piers, who was furtively reaching for yet another small, sugared breadroll from a dish beside the wine-bottle. He was ravenously hungry by now and, regrettably, could think of little else but food. He spluttered on a dry crumb of bread, when the woman added unexpectedly: "And who is this? Your lover?"

"Yes — oh, I must mean *no*!" stammered Louise, colour entering her pale cheeks. "Maman, this is Piers Challis and this is Carrie. Piers brought us here to find you. He is the — the kindest person I have ever had the good fortune to meet," she murmured softly, her eyes downcast.

Piers took a further drink of wine to rid himself of the troublesome crumb.

"I must make use of our meeting, madame," he said, "to inform you that I intend to marry your daughter." His tone was grave, but he had a ridiculous urge to laugh aloud. Perhaps he had been unwise to take wine upon an empty stomach? He added firmly: "We shall be wed when we return home to England."

"Challis? Challis?" pondered Jeannine Latour, as she rolled her glass of wine between her bony hands. "I have heard that name before, *ma fille*."

The woman is as sane as I am, thought Piers thankfully. I have the feeling she does not judge me kindly, after the fear I showed on sight of that knife of hers. I hope she does not expect me to perform some medieval feat of courage to prove my worthiness to wed her daughter! The setting of this ancient castle might be all too appropriate, but unless I am given something more substantial to eat, I shall have strength for nothing!

"Madame la Comtesse knew Sir Reginald Challis before she came to France," explained Louise, her eyes on Piers. "You must have heard her speak his name, Maman. She was to have married Piers' father, you see, and she left him without word when she eloped with Comte Henri. By merest chance, I was cast up on the beach of Challiscombe Bay and have become well-acquainted with the people once known by Madame la Comtesse."

"Chance? Huh?" retorted Jeannine Latour. "It was not chance that you went to this Challiscombe Bay! My husband, Michel, plotted the course with care. Challiscombe Bay was the intended destination. Why did not Michel come back here with you, *ma fille*?"

"He — he was dead when the boat reached England," faltered Louise.

"*Eh bien*, that was Michel all over!" said Jeannine unemotionally. "He never succeeded in anything, that one!"

"Maman," demanded Louise suddenly, "why did he take *me* in the boat, when Héli was still alive? He put her locket, bearing her parents' portraits about my neck and for years I have been uncertain of my own identity."

"M'selle Héli died," said her mother woodenly, "so I urged Michel to take you instead. You too were sired by Comte Henri, *ma fille*."

"Yes, yes, I know that now," said Louise hastily, as she became aware of the little maid, Carrie's startled eyes.

"I must give you the truth," she said at last and motioned that Carrie should sit and listen also. "Héloise-Marie was injured and left for dead. Some time after Michel had left with you, Lucette,

311

I found that she still lived. I nursed her and kept her identity secret even from the good Gaspard Villon. To him, to everyone, she is Marie, the angel of our orphans."

"But does she not question you, madame?" asked Piers reasonably. "Does she accept your authority in what was once her home?"

Jeannine shrugged.

"She knows nothing beyond the fact that she is just Marie," said the woman. "*Ma fille* — did you not see her eyes?"

"Oh — surely Héli is not blind?" gasped Louise in horror.

"Blind? Ah — no, not *blind*," said her mother. "She sees her surroundings and plays with the little ones who call her 'angel'. The blindness is not in her eyes, but in her heart and mind."

"She is not — not *mad*?" faltered Louise

"Mad — sane — who are we to say?" asked Jeannine with a further philosophic shrug. "Her mind has not grown beyond that of a small girl. She sees herself as she was before that day, but she does not ask for her parents. She is sweet-natured and content. She *accepts* — and so must you, *ma fille.*"

"But — but her heritage?" faltered Louise. "She is the last of a noble line — "

"She is Marie, *L'ange aux orphélines!*" stated Jeannine Latour implacably. "I have guarded her from her enemies, from that one who called himself Comte André and I will guard her even from *you*, Lucette! You will not meddle. It is not your concern."

"Comte André?" asked Piers. "So André Durand *did* come here? He came also to Challiscombe, madame. He was seeking a legacy from the past."

"Legacy? Pah!" snorted the woman. "The good Gaspard did not bring Monsieur André into the chateau. He saw only a burnt-out ruin — as *you* would have done, but for Gaspard recognising you as my daughter. What kind of legacy does Monsieur André expect? Does he hope to claim the name of Pont-Rachelle, after all these years?"

"He spoke of a fortune concealed somewhere in the chateau, Maman," whispered Louise. "He was crazed with the idea." She shuddered. "I did not tell you — André Durand is dead!"

"*C'est bien!*" said Jeannine Latour with callous approval. "He would have harmed my Marie, that *canaille*." She paused and thought for a moment before continuing. "*You* also came to claim this legacy, *ma fille*?"

Louise rose to her feet and her blue eyes flashed angrily.

"The sole reason for this journey was to discover if you still lived, Maman!" she said. "You cannot compare *us* with Durand's greed!"

"*Eh bien*." nodded Jeannine, "then I will tell you of the legacy! *Madame la Comtesse* was able to hide a quantity of jewels, but they are no longer in the chateau. We have used them, Marie and I, with the help of the good Gaspard, to feed and clothe our *orphélines*."

"Then we salute you, madame!" agreed Piers gravely. "You have performed a minor miracle, here at Pont-Rachelle."

"I like this lover of yours, *ma fille*," approved Jeannine Latour unsmilingly. "He thinks like a Frenchman!"

"Maman — he is not my l — lover," protested Louise, pressing her hands to her burning cheeks.

"*Comment?* You do not love him? Then you are a fool!" declared this outrageous woman, tossing her irongrey head.

"Love him? Of course I love Piers!" retorted Louise indignantly. "But he is not — we are not — oh, Maman, I think it is your use of English that confuses me."

"My English?" stared Jeannine, affronted. "My command of this barbarous tongue is perfect! Ah, be silent, *ma fille*. You are wasting time! Come — there is something I must show you."

She led them out of her simple,

one-roomed house into the mild warmth of March sunshine. The expanse of green was empty now of children, but the sheep still chewed stolidly at the grass and the lambs were resting now in the shade of a small sapling which had taken root in the old courtyard. Jeannine Latour appeared to be making for one of the chateau's original towers, which formed part of the outer wall of her domain. The ground floor, at least, of this tower, was undamaged.

Piers was heartened to feel Louise clutch his hand and he gave her a reassuring smile.

"I have never before met the like of your mother, love!" he whispered. "It must be she and not Bonaparte who is the mainstay of France!"

Louise tried to show her gratitude for his understanding but her smile did not reach her troubled eyes.

"Miss Louise! Mr. Piers!" said Carrie softly. "You're not to fret I'll tell a single soul of this, when we're home again, but I'm glad I came. I'd not have missed seeing this for *anything*! Madame speaks too strange for me to grasp above half, but I can tell things are all right and that you'm happy to meet your mother again, miss."

Madame Latour beckoned to them impatiently from the open door at the tower's base. Obediently they entered a cold, thick-walled room, only to halt as Jeannine pointed warningly to the floor.

"Our well," she said. "Take care not to fall in, for we rely on the water's purity. Without it, we could not live here. Now, come!"

They went in single file up a twisting stone stair that seemed endless. At last they found themselves in a large, bare room which occupied the entire floor of the tower. Carrie ran to peer from one of the narrow windows.

"I can see the village and the bridge across the stream!" she cried. "Oh, you'm got a splendid look-out here, ma'am!"

Jeannine Latour ignored the maid-servant's childish excitement and turned to face Piers and Louise.

"There is something of interest to you, *m'sieur*," she said to Piers. "You will see why I knew the name of Challis." She removed a loose stone from the tower room's rocky wall and brought out a flat box. For a moment she held the box against her bony chest, then she sighed and opened it. "These papers," she said calmly, "I took from the box that *Madame la Comtesse* asked Michel to take to England. They hold proof of the identity of Héloise-Marie du Pont-Rachelle. When I believed the child to be dead, I hid the papers and gave Michel the empty box and the locket. You may read the papers if you wish, *ma fille*," she went on with a sigh, "but they must not leave the chateau. But *this*, *m'sieur*, you shall take back to England. It is no concern of mine."

Silently, Piers took from her a sealed bundle of papers. Written in a flowing hand beside the seal, he read: "R. Challis, Challis Hall, Devon."

"So Barbara tried to contact my father, after all," he said slowly. "You should not have withheld this letter, madame."

Jeannine Latour shrugged.

"I was with *Madame la Comtesse* when she wrote it, *m'sieur*," she said mildly. "It contains but a plea for him to care for her daughter. I thought Héli was dead and so the letter was unnecessary."

"But you kept it here and did not destroy it?" said Piers evenly.

She shrugged again and gave a grim half-smile.

"Perhaps, *m'sieur*, I knew that one day you would come to Pont-Rachelle?" she suggested.

Piers was saved the necessity of forming a reply, by the entry of Gaspard Villon and an aged white-haired man in a long robe of rusty black.

"You are ready, madame?" asked the old man in French, his voice thin and insubstantial, like the sigh of a breeze through winter's trees.

"Ah, *c'est Monsieur le curé,*" said Jeannine with apparent relief. "Yes, I think there is no more to be said! I am happy to have met you, ma fille," she went on briskly. "You will go back to England now with Monsieur Challis and the little maid. Take the letter to your father, *m'sieur,* and care always for my Lucette. She was sired by a French nobleman and is no peasant, for my own family were respectable farmers in the old days. There is no bad blood in your chosen bride."

She turned away to indicate that the interview was at an end and Louise gasped in disbelief.

"Maman — you wish us to leave now?" she stammered. "But can I not see Héli — I promise not to tell her who she really is. We cannot just *go* as if nothing has happened!"

"What has happened?" retorted Jeannine Latour, seeming to ignore the note of panic in her daughter's voice. "And do not call me *maman, mademoiselle!*

C'est fini — it is over and you must go! I command it! Gaspard — I do not know these people. Take them away, for they are not needed in the *Chateau des Orphélines*!"

On later reflection, Piers Challis saw the wisdom of Madame Latour's decision, but at this moment he was as incredulous and indignant as the trembling Louise. Some of the fire died out of Jeannine's eyes and she looked again at her daughter.

"Maman?" pleaded Louise.

"Go with the *curé* and Gaspard, Lucette," said the woman quietly. "You have achieved your aim. Go back to England and," a glint appeared in her eyes as she added deliberately: "wed your lover."

A long shuddering sigh escaped Louise and she moved to put her lips to her mother's thin cheek, then she took Piers by the hand and nodded to the staring Carrie.

"Come," said Louise clearly. "Come — we must go home."

They followed the old *curé* and the frowning Gaspard Villon from the ancient stone-walled tower-room and Piers looked back to see Jeannine Latour, her hands clenched at her breast and her eyes, no longer wild, filled with an excess of emotion. The difficult decision had shaken even her iron-willed strength of mind. She gave Piers a curt nod and he left her with his most reassuring smile.

They spent the night in Pont-Rachelle, beneath the spotlessly clean roof of Gaspard Villon and the unspoken feeling was one of complete anti-climax. Piers' last waking thought was one of gratitude towards Jeannine Latour. In sending away her daughter, the Frenchwoman had given Louise back to him. When this strange episode was finally at an end, he and Louise would be able to begin their life again — together.

12

THE library of Challis Hall was quiet when Piers fell silent and the eyes of all those present were upon the sealed bundle of papers clutched in the trembling hand of Sir Reginald Challis.

"Perhaps you would prefer to open it when you are alone, Father?" ventured Gerard with an unusual show of tact. "All we need to know is that our travellers are safely home. The letter is for your eyes only."

Sir Reginald shook his greying head.

"It would be churlish of me to withhold the contents of this," he observed, waving the bundle towards his younger son, "when Piers and Louise have risked so much by journeying to France. I have no secrets from my sons, nor from you, Louise and little Milly, for you are already a part of our family."

Gerard smiled and reached for Milly's hand and Piers raised a teasing eyebrow at Louise's customary rise of colour. All was quiet again, except for the crackle of sound as Sir Reginald broke the seal and spread the wad of closely-written pages on his knee. His eyes ran swiftly down each page in turn and he grunted and nodded to himself.

"Yes," he said at length. "Barbara intended that this should have accompanied her daughter to England. She wished me to convey the child, Héloise-Marie, to her grandparents and to explain that *she* was unavoidably prevented from coming herself — "

"Oh, sir," murmured gentle Milly Parswell with a sigh. "She was very brave, your Barbara."

They all pondered on the unexpected knowledge of the bravery of Barbara Trevanny, who had chosen to stay in France and meet the same fate as her husband upon the guillotine.

"Barbara says she was to put the

letter in a box, together with jewellery, to be sure that the child did not arrive here penniless. She speaks of her trust in one Michel Latour who is confident of his ability to bring a boat directly into our bay."

"Jeannine Latour spoke of no jewellery, other than the locket," frowned Piers, nodding to the golden trinket on the arm of his father's chair.

Louise spoke then, her voice quiet but firm.

"My mother must have removed the jewellery from the box," she said. "At that time she thought that little Héli was dead and would have judged it theft to send anything of value with me, when I took Héli's place in the boat."

"I would have liked to have met this mother of yours, my dear," said Sir Reginald regretfully. "From all you tell me, she possesses great integrity."

"Her daughter has inherited much of her mother's strength of character," said Piers, no longer smiling. "Yes, Louise," he added, "I am serious for once! You have an inner strength on which we all rely. If you had been an ordinary unimaginative child, you would never have risen beyond the confines of your life with old Caleb Vaughan."

"Do not minimise the effect that old man had upon my life, Piers," pleaded Louise. "He took me in and protected me and because of his kindness he — he died." She turned to Sir Reginald and went on: "André Durand boasted of attacking that frightened old man, sir. I must tell you that he also boasted of shooting you, that night upon the beach. He killed poor harmless Raymond Beckwith so that the blame for your injury would rest upon him. Beckwith was never a smuggler! André was completely obsessed with his desire for a legacy from Pont-Rachelle and he saw you, sir, as a barrier to his aim. He wanted you dead or incapacitated, so that he might discover whether I or even Milly could be his sought-for Héloise-Marie."

"He even wondered if *I* could be this girl?" asked Milly with round eyes. "But, Louise, you never spoke a word of it to me!"

"I left Challiscombe with him so that you would all be safe from his intentions," whispered Louise. "But I was not brave — not brave like Comtesse Barbara! Her conduct puts my own poor effort to shame!"

"That fellow Durand died without learning the irony of the use to which his supposed legacy had been put!" realised Gerard suddenly, with a shake of his head. "All the while he was out hunting those jewels, they were being used for needy orphans! There is a jest, if ever one existed!" His smile faded when he added remorsefully: "And *I* was the fool who set myself beneath Durand's thumb and put Louise at risk. I deserve to be horse-whipped!"

"As my mother told us," said Louise slowly, "that is all over now. The future is the important thing — not the dead past. I realise that now, Piers," she admitted, when the younger twin pressed her hand comfortingly. "I will never again cause you another moment's distress. I promise you!"

"Do not promise to be dull, love!" protested Piers. "The future that I plan for us excludes all dullness!"

She turned her shining eyes upon him and was saved from replying by a puzzled exclamation from Sir Reginald, who was still pursuing the closely-written lines of his letter.

"Well, here is an oddity!" declared the elderly gentleman. "Barbara writes here of her hope that I forgave her when I read her note of explanation and saw that she had returned all but the locket from the gifts I bestowed upon her." He looked up dazedly. "But I never received either the note or the jewels." he protested. "I thought she left me without a word — ah, yes! She writes here of my knowledge of the chosen hiding-place."

He rose to his feet and groaned aloud.

"What is wrong, Father?" asked Gerard.

"I condemned her as heartless, when all the while her note and jewels were waiting to be discovered, here in Challis Hall," said his father, as he moved to stand in front of the painted likeness of Barbara Trevanny, the portrait which had spent long years turned to the wall. "See," said Sir Reginald, "she put them in the place we always used when we exchanged secret notes."

He pushed at a panel of the wall beside the picture and a small concealed cupboard opened with a click.

"You never told *us* about a secret compartment!" accused Gerard.

"Are the jewels there?" asked Piers.

Slowly their father withdrew a cloth-wrapped bundle, which fell open to reveal a quantity of jewellery and a folded paper.

"*This* note I must read alone," declared Sir Reginald and his eyes were suspiciously wet. "I misjudged you so unfairly, Barbara," he told her smiling, uncaring portrait.

Tactfully the twins and their ladies left the elderly gentleman with the relics of his lost love. Gerard and Milly went out to walk in the garden, beneath the welcome spring sunshine. Piers led Louise purposefully towards the drawing-room, where they could be reasonably sure of being uninterrupted for a time. This lengthy pursuit of a legacy which had proved so elusive, was finally at an end. Only the future was important now.

★ ★ ★

The uneasy peace with France was over. In May of that year of 1803, war was again declared and a beacon was built on the cliff-top above Challiscombe Bay, to be lit if invasion by the French was imminent.

The early months of this new war claimed as victim the military brother of Cousin Marianne's 'impoverished curate'. Through this unhappy circumstance, Marianne's betrothed inherited his family's wealth and was now able to support a wife. Thomas Challis breathed a sigh of relief. With his remaining daughter provided for, he found it was now possible to fulfil his dearest wish, by making his nephew, Piers, sole heir to his considerable estate in Yorkshire.

Louise and Piers were married in that first summer of the renewed war and travelled north to make their home with Uncle Thomas, at the old man's express desire. Sir Reginald could find no fault with this plan, for his younger son promised to visit Challiscombe whenever occasion arose.

When Gerard wed his gentle Milly, the vicar was left without a housekeeper. It seemed both fair and natural that this position should be offered to Annis Beckwith, who had been so cruelly widowed by André Durand. Little Carrie left the vicar's service at her own request and became personal maid to her Miss Louise in Yorkshire.

It was Gerard Challis who travelled to Cornwall in search of the parents of the dead Barbara Trevanny. Through these old people, the final thread in the tangled web of André Durand's obsession lay revealed. The past was now truly dead and laid to rest. As Jeannine Latour, at peace with her *orphélines*, had so accurately declared:

"*C'est fini!* It is over!"

THE END

Other titles in the
Linford Romance Library:

A YOUNG MAN'S FANCY
Nancy Bell

Six people get together for reasons of their own, and the result is one of misunderstanding, suspicion and mounting tension.

THE WISDOM OF LOVE
Janey Blair

Barbie meets Louis and receives flattering proposals, but her reawakened affection for Jonah develops into an overwhelming passion.

MIRAGE IN THE MOONLIGHT
Mandy Brown

En route to an island to be secretary to a multi-millionaire, Heather's stubborn loyalty to her former flatmate plunges her into a grim hazard.

WITH SOMEBODY ELSE
Theresa Charles

Rosamond sets off for Cornwall with Hugo to meet his family, blissfully unaware of the shocks in store for her.

A SUMMER FOR STRANGERS
Claire Hamilton

Because she had lost her job, her flat and she had no money, Tabitha agreed to pose as Adam's future wife although she believed the scheme to be deceitful and cruel.

VILLA OF SINGING WATER
Angela Petron

The disquieting incidents that occurred at the Vatican and the Colosseum did not trouble Jan at first, but then they became increasingly unpleasant and alarming.

DOCTOR NAPIER'S NURSE
Pauline Ash

When cousins Midge and Derry are entered as probationer nurses on the same day but at different hospitals they agree to exchange identities.

A GIRL LIKE JULIE
Louise Ellis

Caroline absolutely adored Hugh Barrington, but then Julie Crane came into their lives. Julie was the kind of girl who attracts men without even trying.

COUNTRY DOCTOR
Paula Lindsay

When Evan Richmond bought a practice in a remote country village he did not realise that a casual encounter would lead to the loss of his heart.

ENCORE
Helga Moray

Craig and Janet realise that their true happiness lies with each other, but it is only under traumatic circumstances that they can be reunited.

NICOLETTE
Ivy Preston

When Grant Alston came back into her life, Nicolette was faced with a dilemma. Should she follow the path of duty or the path of love?

THE GOLDEN PUMA
Margaret Way

Catherine's time was spent looking after her father's Queensland farm. But what life was there without David, who wasn't interested in her?

HOSPITAL BY THE LAKE
Anne Durham

Nurse Marguerite Ingleby was always ready to become personally involved with her patients, to the despair of Brian Field, the Senior Surgical Registrar, who loved her.

VALLEY OF CONFLICT
David Farrell

Isolated in a hostel in the French Alps, Ann Russell sees her fiancé being seduced by a young girl. Then comes the avalanche that imperils their lives.

NURSE'S CHOICE
Peggy Gaddis

A proposal of marriage from the incredibly handsome and wealthy Reagan was enough to upset any girl — and Brooke Martin was no exception.

A DANGEROUS MAN
Anne Goring

Photographer Polly Burton was on safari in Mombasa when she met enigmatic Leon Hammond. But unpredictability was the name of the game where Leon was concerned.

PRECIOUS INHERITANCE
Joan Moules

Karen's new life working for an authoress took her from Sussex to a foreign airstrip and a kidnapping; to a real life adventure as gripping as any in the books she typed.

VISION OF LOVE
Grace Richmond

When Kathy takes over the rundown country kennels she finds Alec Stinton, a local vet, very helpful. But their friendship arouses bitter jealousy and a tragedy seems inevitable.

HEART OF ICE
Marie Sidney

How was January to know that not only would the warmth of the Swiss people thaw out her frozen heart, but that she too would play her part in helping someone to live again?

LUCKY IN LOVE
Margaret Wood

Companion-secretary to wealthy gambler Laura Duxford, who lived in Monaco, seemed to Melanie a fabulous job. Especially as Melanie had already lost her heart to Laura's son, Julian.

NURSE TO PRINCESS JASMINE
Lilian Woodward

Nick's surgeon brother, Tom, performs an operation on an Arabian princess, and she invites Tom, Nick and his fiancé to Omander, where a web of deceit and intrigue closes about them.

THE WAYWARD HEART
Eileen Barry

Disaster-prone Katherine's nick-name was 'Kate Calamity', but her boss went too far with an outrageous proposal, which because of her latest disaster, she could not refuse.

FOUR WEEKS IN WINTER
Jane Donnelly

Tessa wasn't looking forward to meeting Paul Mellor again — she had made a fool of herself over him once before. But was Orme Jared's solution to her problem likely to be the right one?

SURGERY BY THE SEA
Sheila Douglas

Medical student Meg hadn't really wanted to go and work with a G.P. on the Welsh coast although the job had its compensations. But Owen Roberts was certainly not one of them!

HEAVEN IS HIGH
Anne Hampson

The new heir to the Manor of Marbeck had been found. But it was rather unfortunate that when he arrived unexpectedly he found an uninvited guest, complete with stetson and high boots.

LOVE WILL COME
Sarah Devon

June Baker's boss was not really her idea of her ideal man, but when she went from third typist to boss's secretary overnight she began to change her mind.

ESCAPE TO ROMANCE
Kay Winchester

Oliver and Jean first met on Swale Island. They were both trying to begin their lives afresh, but neither had bargained for complications from the past.

CASTLE IN THE SUN
Cora Mayne

Emma's invalid sister, Kym, needed a warm climate, and Emma jumped at the chance of a job on a Mediterranean island. But Emma soon finds that intrigues and hazards lurk on the sunlit isle.

BEWARE OF LOVE
Kay Winchester

Carol Brampton resumes her nursing career when her family is killed in a car accident. With Dr. Patrick Farrell she begins to pick up the pieces of her life, but is bitterly hurt when insinuations are made about her to Patrick.

DARLING REBEL
Sarah Devon

When Jason Farradale's secretary met with an accident, her glamorous stand-in was quite unable to deal with one problem in particular.

THE PRICE OF PARADISE
Jane Arbor

It was a shock to Fern to meet her estranged husband on an island in the middle of the Indian Ocean, but to discover that her father had engineered it puzzled Fern. What did he hope to achieve?

DOCTOR IN PLASTER
Lisa Cooper

When Dr. Scott Sutcliffe is injured, Nurse Caroline Hurst has to cope with a very demanding private case. But when she realises her exasperating patient has stolen her heart, how can Caroline possibly stay?

A TOUCH OF HONEY
Lucy Gillen

Before she took the job as secretary to author Robert Dean, Cadie had heard how charming he was, but that wasn't her first impression at all.

ROMANTIC LEGACY
Cora Mayne
As kennelmaid to the Armstrongs, Ann Brown, had no idea that she would become the central figure in a web of mystery and intrigue.

THE RELENTLESS TIDE
Jill Murray
Steve Palmer shared Nurse Marie Blane's love of the sea and small boats. Marie's other passion was her step-brother. But when danger threatened who should she turn to — her step-brother or the man who stirred emotions in her heart?

ROMANCE IN NORWAY
Cora Mayne
Nancy Crawford hopes that her visit to Norway will help her to start life again. She certainly finds many surprises there, including unexpected happiness.

SHADOW DANCE
Margaret Way

When Carl Danning sent her to interview Richard Kauffman, Alix was far from pleased — but the assignment led her to help Richard repair the situation between him and his ex-wife.

WHITE HIBISCUS
Rosemary Pollock

'A boring English model with dubious morals,' was how Count Paul Santana Demajo described Emma. But what about the Count's morals, and who is Marianne?

STARS THROUGH THE MIST
Betty Neels

Secretly in love with Gerard van Doordninck, Deborah should have been thrilled when he asked her to marry him. But he only wanted a wife for practical not romantic reasons.

UNLOCK MY HEART
Honor Vincent

When Ruth Linton, a young widow with three children, inherits a house in the country, it seems to be the answer to her dreams. But Ruth's problems were only just beginning . . .

SWEET PROMISE
Janet Dailey

Erica had met Rafael in Mexico, where their relationship had been brief but dramatic. Now, over a year later in Texas, she had met him again — and he had the power to wreck her life.

SAFARI ENCOUNTER
Rosemary Carter

Jenny had to accept that she couldn't run her father's game park alone; so she let forceful Joshua Adams virtually take over. But Joshua took over her heart as well!